Sophie pulled her arm away from Seth's grasp. 'Thank you very much. It was interesting meeting you. I dare say——?'

It was another sentence she did not finish. As she pulled back he caught her fingers, then abruptly pulled her to him, into his arms, and kissed her hard and passionately. It was a raw, physical embrace, and his hands shifted under her jacket, and up over the nakedness of her back, possessing her warm skin.

For the briefest moment a swift unbidden shaft of desire arrowed through the heart of her, then it was gone, pushed out by an overwhelming tide of outrage at what he was doing. She flung her head to one side.

'Stop it! How dare you?'

She tried to push him away from her, but his chest was like iron. Only when he finally chose to drop his arms was she released.

His hair was tousled and his breath uneven, but he did not look in the slightest bit abashed by his behaviour. His eyes were warm, alive.

'What the hell do you think you're doing?'

He ran a hand through his hair, his mouth crooking cruelly.

'I thought, since I was the wolf, I'd better behave true to character.'

BITTER SECRET

BY

CAROL GREGOR

MILLS & BOON LIMITED
ETON HOUSE   18-24 PARADISE ROAD
RICHMOND   SURREY   TW9 1SR

First published in Great Britain 1989 by Mills & Boon Limited

© Carol Gregor 1989

Australian copyright 1989 Philippine copyright 1989 This edition 1989

ISBN 0 263 76442 7

Set in Plantin 11 on 11½ pt. 01–8910–48627

Typeset in Great Britain by JCL Graphics, Bristol

Made and Printed in Great Britain

CHAPTER ONE

'SOPHIE, darling, at last! Although at least you've come. I was beginning to wonder——'

'I'm sorry, Amanda, I really am. But one of the children had an accident in the playground this afternoon. I had to go to the hospital to see how he was. I tried to ring you from there, but the telephone was out of order.'

'Oh, dear,' Amanda drawled, 'nothing serious, I hope?'

'No, thank goodness. He hit his head, but it's only mild concussion, nothing worse.'

'Good, good.' Amanda wasn't listening, she could tell. 'Well, now you're finally here, you'd better hurry on in and meet everyone. Although I suppose you'll need to titivate first.'

Sophie stepped out of the darkness into the hall and felt Amanda's keen glance take in every detail of her appearance. She pulled a face. 'Do I look that awful?'

Amanda looked with scarcely hidden envy over her guest's luminous skin, her soft natural curls of honey and ash, and bewitching smoky blue eyes. 'You look as ravishing as ever, Sophie. You know, I know women who would kill for your looks, yet you seem to take them for granted.'

She shrugged, saying, 'I've never known anything different,' and turned to smile at the village girl who

had hurried forward to take her coat. 'Hello, Tracey.
Are you on dinner duty tonight? How's young Glenn
getting on at his new school?'

'Fine, miss, thank you.' The girl's shy, rural vowels
contrasted strongly with Amanda's social drawl.

'Does he actually manage to get up in time to catch
the bus?'

Tracey smiled. 'Mum bangs a pan by his 'ead until
he can't stand it any more. Then he has to get up.'

Behind her she heard taffeta flounces rustle
impatiently. Quickly she handed over her jacket,
saying, 'I'll just slip into the cloakroom for a minute.
Don't wait, Amanda, I'll come straight in,' and she
escaped through the nearby door. In the quiet she
stood for a moment or two putting herself in the right
frame of mind for the grand dinner party ahead. She
repaired her lipstick and repinned the combs that held
her curls back from her fine cheekbones, then
smoothed down the narrow sheath of black velvet over
her slender hips and grimaced.

The dress looked stunning, but it had been a
mistake to buy it. Hurrying late into town last
weekend, she had had a desperate search for
something—anything—she could wear tonight.

When she slipped the simple black dress on it had
felt wonderful, and after a hasty twist in front of the
mirror she had shrugged it off and written out the
horribly large cheque needed to buy it.

Only when she got home and tried it on at leisure
had she realised just how low-cut and revealing its off-
the-shoulder top was, how clinging the skirt.
Although she loved clothes and wore them with flair,
she never wore things so blatantly sexual. And

although her figure, both full and slender, was perfect
for the dress, the glamorous seductress who stared
back at her from the mirror was a stranger to her
eyes.

She sighed, and picked up her bag. It was done now.
Too late to worry. She would just have to brazen it
out.

Outside the door she met Amanda, still hovering.

'My goodness, Sophie! That's—incredible.'

'Well, different, anyway. Actually I hate it. I want
to keep pulling it up. I feel half-naked.'

'You are,' Amanda said bluntly. 'But you look
fantastic. They aren't going to know what's hit them.
Come on.' She was already tapping her way across the
entrance hall to the double-panelled doors. 'I've got
the most perfect man for you to meet.'

'I doubt it,' said Sophie softly as she followed
Amanda in. She had met dozens of 'perfect' men at
Amanda's famed dinner parties and not one of them
had been the sort she wanted to see again once the
evening was over.

In fact she often wondered why she continued to
accept invitations to evenings at Bicknor Manor when
she had so little in common with Tim and Amanda
and their relentless socialising. Often she was tempted
to ring up at the last minute with some excuse or
other. But the moment the door opened on to a blaze
of warmth and colour, and a happy hubbub of talk,
she remembered exactly why.

Her eyes feasted on the beauty of the rich Persian
carpets, the velvet curtains, the roaring logs in the
enormous carved fireplace. Tim, Amanda's husband,
looked her over with open appreciation as he handed

her a drink, and the cut glass sparkled in her hand and the sherry was rich and smooth.

Such opulence was worlds away from her usual hard-working life, but that was exactly why she enjoyed it so much, she thought, as she sank quietly down into a corner of a deep sofa. She liked good food and drink, and although her fellow guests were rarely to her taste, she enjoyed meeting new faces.

Normally, too, she loved the chance to dress up for the evening, and since she knew only too well that her role at the Manor's polished mahogany dining-table was mainly a decorative one, she had no hesitation in doing her best to look as beautiful as she knew how. But tonight her appearance gave her no pleasure and she sipped her sherry quickly, hoping it would smooth away her uncomfortableness, as well as ease the tiredness of her long and difficult week. It did, and she began to feel better.

Amanda had given her a moment or two to collect her thoughts, but now she leant down and introduced her to an elderly man sitting near her. He was a cordial but painstakingly slow conversationalist, and after a moment or two her glance began to stray discreetly round the room.

It did not get far. There, leaning languidly against the mantelpiece, was the most striking man she had ever seen in her life. And he was looking at her. No, not looking. He was stripping her naked, devouring her with his eyes, quite openly and without any hint of shame!

The look drove all thoughts from her head. She completely lost the thread of what the elderly gentleman was saying. She had heard of smouldering glances. This one was a blaze, as much a conflagration as the fire he stood beside.

She could not look away. She swallowed. She felt his eyes on her skin, like an intimate caress of her neck and shoulders. Beneath her dress her body lifted and tightened towards him.

Her hand shook and spilled some of her drink. He had noticed. He began to smile, lazily, conspiratorially, one side of his mouth crooking more deeply than the other. She looked away, then back. Now the glass as slippery in her shaking hand. She leaned forward to put it down on the coffee-table beside her, but before she got it there it slipped from her grasp, struck the glass table top and shattered on to the Persian rug.

Everyone in the room stopped talking. It was so embarrassing, she felt herself flushing. Then the man crossed the room and was swiftly picking up the pieces.

'Don't worry, Seth. Tracey will see to it,' Amanda instructed and went to summon the girl. The conversations around the room resumed.

'I always have thought glass coffee-tables were lethal objects,' the man said to her, and he looked up at her with wicked, laughing eyes.

'It was nothing to do with the table!' she hissed fiercely.

'Oh?' He paused in his ministrations, kneeling on one knee and stared, mockingly inquisitive, at her. Now he was very close.

'You made me do it. You know you did.'

'Me?' He was enjoying himself. 'I was on the other side of the room. I'm not a magician.'

'Looking at me like that.'

'A cat can look at a king.'

'Not looking, then, leering.'

'I can promise you I've never leered in my life. Dirty old men in raincoats leer. I was, I admit, looking. But why shouldn't a normal, warm-blooded male look at the female form? Especially,' he lowered his voice, 'when it is so delicious, and so utterly exposed as yours.'

She sat back quickly, acutely aware that as she leaned down towards him she was even more exposed than the dramatic dress intended.

She glared at him fiercely, unaware that her anger only made her eyes smoke more luminously and sent a perfect flush of colour along her fine high cheekbones. From the smirk on his face she guessed he thought he had won the point.

'Most normal warm-blooded males have seen enough low-cut dresses not to behave like eye-popping schoolboys every time they set eyes on them,' she persisted. He rattled her and she was not going to let him see it.

'Every time?' He levered himself up and sat easily next to her on the long sofa. The old gentleman at the far end had long ago turned his attention elsewhere. 'Who said anything about every time? In my life—which I willingly admit has seen more decadence than many—I've probably viewed more low-cut dresses than you've had hot dinners. Not to mention,' his eyes went outrageously over her again, 'more tiny waists, more long, slim legs in sheer black stockings, more slender ankles. Very few even make me want to glance twice any more. You can stand assured you rated very special treatment.'

''Scuse me, miss.' Tracey had arrived with dustpan and brush to clear away the damage.

'Miss?' The man burst into astonished laughter. 'With that dress, wouldn't madam be more appropriate?'

'Oh!' Sophie gasped in an outrage of disbelief. 'How dare you?' Tracey stood open-mouthed, awkwardly wondering what she had done that was so funny. The girl's bafflement redoubled Sophie's anger at this man, this stranger, who seemed to care not a jot for anyone's feelings but his own.

'It's all right, Tracey,' she said swiftly, gently. 'He's not laughing at you.' She shot him a savage glance, and he had the grace to look marginally abashed.

At that moment, Tim summoned them all in to dinner. 'Ah, Seth, Sophie,' he boomed, vaguely, 'see you've already—yes, yes—well, come on in.'

Seth stood and offered her his arm. 'I guess from that incoherent mumble that I'm destined to lead you to the trough. Will you do me the honour of accompanying me? If I promise not to look down your frock once?'

Despite herself she laughed. She did not mean to, but his irreverence pricked the usual pomposity of evenings like this in a not unwelcome way. And when she took the crook of his arm to walk through to the dining-room she was acutely aware of the warmth and ease of his long, lean body beside her.

They were seated opposite each other at the table. Branching silver candlesticks with cream tapers lit the table and threw their reflections into deep pools on the dark polished wood. As he opened his napkin and tossed cheerful remarks to the guests on each side of

him she was able to scrutinise him closely for the first
time.

That first, startling impression had simply been of
his challenging maleness. Now she saw he was a tall
man, whose broad shoulders wore his dark dinner
jacket lightly. The whiteness of his shirt emphasised
his light tan and the thick depths of his chestnut hair.

She had thought his eyes were brown, like his hair,
but now she saw that was only partly true. As he
laughed and spoke, she saw they contained a
fascinating blend of other colours—gold and green
and grey. She looked closer and closer, almost
hypnotised by their complex depths, then she started
and recollected herself enough to sip at the cucumber
and lobster soup.

For a time she did her social duty, exchanging light
pleasantries with her neighbours, a middle-aged
merchant banker and the wife of a local solicitor, but
her eyes were constantly pulled back to him. His face
was expressive, warm, full of humour. He had such
presence that both his neighbours were delighting in
his company, and it seemed for all the world that he
had quite forgotten her. It gave her the chance to
study his features, the dark brows, strong cheekbones
and straight lips, but it also made her feel strangely
peeved.

Then, as she looked at him, his eyes went swiftly to
hers, as if he had been aware of her all along, and he
smiled slowly and so directly sensually at her that for
a moment a private world of desire and longing
seemed to rise up and unfold them both.

Amanda's voice from down the table broke the
spell, and Sophie was relieved. She did not want these

feelings, they had no place in her life any more, and
they made her feel frightened and lost.

'Sophie, darling, forgive me. But you arrived so
very late there was no time to make proper
introductions.'

'Ouch,' said a low voice to her across the table.

'Seth Huntingdon, Sophie Walker.' Amanda leaned
forward. 'I so much wanted you two to meet. Sophie's
a keen member of the local Conservation Society,
Seth. I'm sure she'll be fascinated to hear your plans
for Sedbury Hall.'

Their neighbours laughed.

'Sounds like "a lively exchange of views" coming
up!' said the merchant banker.

'So it's you who bought the Hall!' the solicitor's
wife said. 'According to the local paper you're an
international property developer. Is that right? People
are so rude about property developers that I've always
longed to meet one.'

He laughed. ' "If you cut us, do we not bleed?" ' he
quoted, hand on his heart.

His fingers were long and straight, Sophie noticed,
with firm, blunt nails. She shook her head slightly and
asked, more sharply than she had intended, 'And just
what *are* your plans for Sedbury Hall?'

He leant back and surveyed her in a calculating
manner for a moment. 'I can assure you, you won't
like them.'

'Perhaps I could be the judge of that.'

'We-ell.' He put his fingertips together and looked
at her over the top of them, choosing his words. 'You
have to acknowledge we live in a leisure society.' She
nodded, reluctantly, feeling the hateful jargon harsh

on her ears. 'So it seems to me that what people want is a multi-functional complex that will answer their business needs while also affording them the chance to relax in a non-stressful environment.'

Surely he couldn't be serious? Her eyes flickered over him, but there was no mockery in his eyes and his tone was serious.

She put her knife and fork down, suddenly not hungry any more. The poached turbot could have been sawdust for all she could taste.

'You mean——'

'Oh, I haven't decided on the final details,' he said, waving away her interruption. 'There's still the dry rot and wet rot and new floors and ceilings to deal with. But I thought something like a combination business centre, health farm and sports centre. I could get a spa pool and jacuzzi complex out of the main bedrooms, with beauty-treatment rooms off the gallery. There could be a fully equipped gym in the stables and a snooker-room in the old kitchens. All the rooms will have wall-size video screens, of course, and there'll be a communications centre in the library. There should be plenty of room for computer terminals and fax machines once we tear out that musty old panelling.'

'What about outside?' she got out.

'I thought a practice golf course on the back terrace and perhaps an all-weather plastic dome over an outdoor pool. The hill behind the house would make a good motor-cycle scrambling track, but I'm not sure that's quite the clientele I'm after——'

'You'll never get planning permission!' Sophie exploded. Sedbury Hall was a fine old Elizabethan house, set high above a neighbouring village in a beautiful bowl of hills. It had been empty for years, left to decay while its owner made his fortune in Australian gold, but he had died, and the recent sale of the house had raised local hopes that it might be lovingly restored.

'I wouldn't be so sure of that. It's in such a bad state that if my plans fall by the wayside it's likely to have to come down. Anyway,' he flashed a brilliant smile at the solicitor's wife, 'we property developers have ways of getting things done, as I'm sure you've heard.' He rubbed his fingers together. 'Money always talks.'

'Oh!' Sophie was repulsed by what she heard, and appalled that she could have felt any pull of attraction to a man like this. 'Not everyone's like that!' Like you, she meant. 'And it would never be pulled down. The National Trust would buy it, if they had to.'

'Would they? They're turning properties down every day of the week. They can hardly afford to maintain the ones they have got. The Hall is a pretty little house, but it's not that exceptional. I'll promise to keep the front façade intact and that'll keep the planners quite happy, you mark my words.'

He smiled brilliantly at her again, but now she was unmoved by his charm.

'It might keep the planners happy. I wouldn't be so sure about everyone else. There will be a tremendous local outcry.'

If anything, his smile broadened. 'Is that a threat I hear? I do so hope so. If there's one thing I enjoy it's a good hard fight.'

She smiled tightly back. 'I can promise you I'll do the best I possibly can to make sure you get what you want.' And with that she turned pointedly away and ignored him for the rest of the evening.

It was late by the time the party finally began to break up, and Sophie's head was pounding with tiredness as she shrugged her jacket over her hateful dress and made her way across the gravel drive. Cold rain poured down on her and when she turned the ignition key in her car the engine only coughed and spluttered in the damp.

'Damn and blast!'

'Such language—from a conservationist.'

She got out, slamming the door, and felt her high heels digging into the wet drive. Seth had followed her closely out of the front door and paused to observe her misfortune. Now he walked quickly over and dived under her bonnet. She shivered as he unclipped wires and ministered to her sickly engine with a handkerchief that he pulled from his pocket.

'Try that.'

The engine still sputtered sadly.

'Sorry. Can't help you any further, I'm afraid. It's well and truly soaked. You'll have to leave it to dry out.'

'That's no problem. I can walk. It's no distance.'

'In this weather? Nonsense. My carriage awaits.' He indicated a smart black Range Rover.

'It would only take five minutes,' she protested.

'In those shoes it would take you five minutes to get to the end of the drive. By which time you would look like a drowned rat.'

He had a point. She got in, slamming the door hard and rudely neglecting to thank him. He climbed into the driving-seat beside her. The dark vehicle seemed uncomfortably intimate. He turned and grinned at her.

'Into the lair of the enemy,' he intoned dramatically, and started the engine.

'Which way are you going?' she said stiffly.

'Whichever way you want.'

'I meant, which way would you be going?'

'To Sedbury, of course.'

She was surprised, she did not think the Hall was habitable in its present state, but she was determined to ask no questions, to build no links of friendship between them.

'Then you'll be going past the end of my road. It's on the other edge of the village. You can drop me at the turning.'

In silence they drove through the main street, where all the houses were in darkness. She stifled a yawn, longing for the shelter of home and bed, and for the whole upsetting evening to be over.

'Here it is.'

'I'll take you to your door.'

She was firm. 'There's absolutely no need. It's less than a hundred yards.'

'It's the middle of the night.'

'It's the middle of rural Gloucestershire. Nothing is going to happen to me.'

'Ah. Remember Little Red Riding Hood? In the forest? That was pretty rural, too.'

'The only wolf around here——' She bit back her words, but the end of her sentence hung clearly between them. He did not turn to look at her but she saw he was grinning wickedly as he pulled into the side.

He got out and came round to open the door. In the darkness he was just a shimmer of black and white, dark hair and eyes and dinner suit, white shirt and teeth. He helped her down, a hand on her elbow. She could feel the power of him, the mischief, as she landed beside him and she shivered deeply. She had been right, he was a real wolf, and he made her very edgy.

She pulled her arm away from his grasp. 'Thank you very much. It was interesting meeting you. I dare say——'

It was another sentence she did not finish. As she pulled back he caught her fingers, then abruptly pulled her to him, into his arms, and kissed her hard and passionately. It was a raw, physical embrace, so forceful she was pushed hard up against the side of the Range Rover while he bruised her mouth with his searching, wanting lips, and his hands shifted under her jacket, and up over the nakedness of her back, possessing her warm skin.

For the briefest moment a swift unbidden shaft of desire arrowed through the heart of her, then it was gone, pushed out by an overwhelming tide of outrage at what he was doing. She flung her head to one side, her lips tearing savagely from his mouth.

'Stop it! How dare you?'

She tried to push him away from her, but his chest was like iron. Only when he finally chose to drop his arms was she released.

His hair was tousled and his breath uneven, but he did not look in the slightest bit abashed by his behaviour. His eyes were warm, alive.

'What the hell do you think you're doing?'

He ran a hand through his hair, his mouth crooking cruelly.

'I thought, since I was the wolf, I'd better behave true to character,' he drawled, then with a grin and a lift of his hand in farewell he jumped into his Range Rover and sped off into the night.

CHAPTER TWO

THE RAIN had stopped, and the morning sun was climbing past Sophie's bedroom window. Outside the birds sang so loudly they seemed to be echoing inside her head.

She groaned, punched her pillow, then stuck her head beneath it. Her temples pounded. She must have drunk far more of Tim's fine claret last night than she had realised. That was the trouble with letting go after a hard and difficult week, she thought. Once you started to unwind, you quickly began to unravel completely.

Now the sun had found a crack in her defences and was making her eyelids glare red. She gave up the struggle to sleep and pushed herself up against the pillows. It wasn't only her head that hurt, she realised; her lips felt sore and bruised as well. Then she remembered, all in one rushing go.

'Oh!' she groaned again as the anger and humiliation of last night flooded back to her. She fingered her lips and grimaced at the tenderness of her swollen flesh.

So she hadn't imagined the force of that uninvited embrace. She really had been kissed so hard that the damage was still there to see this morning. The man was outrageous! A monster!

She shut her eyes again, remembering everything

about Seth Huntingdon, from that first insolent stare
to the way he had pushed her back against his Range
Rover to plunder her lips.

He was worse than a monster. He was a raper and
pillager! When he saw something he wanted, whether
it was a woman or a house, he just walked right in and
took it. She loathed the very thought of him.

The sound of a car engine interrupted her thoughts.
She frowned. Hardly anyone came up this tiny cul-de-
sac, and certainly not first thing on Saturday morning.
Although—she squinted at her clock—perhaps half
past ten was not exactly the crack of dawn.

Then her doorbell rang. She got up and, pushing
back the curtains, saw an unknown white van outside.
Pulling on her dressing-gown, she hurried downstairs.

'Miss Walker?'

'Yes.'

'Oh, good. Flowers for you. I was given the road,
but not the number. I had to look you up in the phone
book. Glad I've got the right house.'

'Oh! Thank you.' It was the largest bunch of red
roses she had ever seen in her life. Her arms hardly
went round them. She went to the kitchen and put
them in water, and, peeling off the white envelope,
went slowly back up the bed.

The message was short and to the point: 'With
apologies from a contrite wolf.' No signature. She
threw it down. She would have liked to be able to
believe it, but she simply didn't. It was just another
move in his game. She was a prize his eye had
happened upon, and she sensed he would do anything
to get it.

She remembered his gesture at the dinner table last

night, the cynical proffering of imaginary bank notes. Everyone had their price, he had implied, and now he was trying to find hers.

Well, he wouldn't find it, because she did not have one. She wasn't interested in him, or any other man, not in any way.

She got up and brushed her hair up into a sensible morning ponytail and pulled on her weekend jeans and white sweatshirt.

Her headache was clearing rapidly, so it could not have been the wine, she thought, as she took her coffee outside to feel the blessing of the spring sun on her face. Instead it must have been the way she had slept, deeply and suffocatingly, wrapped up under the covers like a terrified schoolgirl. She sat down on her back step and rested her chin in her hands, confronting uncomfortable thoughts. There was something she had not let herself remember about last night, but the knowledge of it buzzed in her brain like an angry bee.

Now she faced it. The truth was, Seth Huntingdon had had a deeply disturbing effect on her. She didn't like him, she hated what he stood for, and she most certainly did not want to have anything to do with him. And yet she would be less than honest if she did not admit that he had roused her senses in a way that no one had done for years, and that her first instinctive response to his embrace had been a searing moment of mindless, yielding desire.

It was that that had sent her running for the cover of drugged sleep, and set her head pounding with tension. Because she had thought that side of her life quite finished, and she wanted nothing to disturb the painful black ghosts that she had long ago shut behind barred and shuttered doors in her mind.

She got up quickly and went back into the house, and her foot kicked against the bucket of roses. Should they go in the dustbin? She bent and looked into their perfect hearts and decided they were too beautiful to waste on such a pointless gesture. After all, Seth Huntingdon would never know, one way or the other, what she had done with his flowers, since she planned never to let him set foot past her door.

She sought solace in hard physical activity, drawn out into her tiny garden by the warm spring weather. By lunch time she had worked round all her flower-beds and even given the lawn its first mow of the season. She rubbed her nose with the back of a muddy hand and surveyed her kingdom with pride. After three years, the garden she had so carefully planned and planted was finally coming to maturity.

'Very nice. But you've missed that bit of grass under the apple tree.'

She whirled around.

'You! What the hell do you think you're doing, coming here?'

He had come down the path at the side of the house and was now standing, quite relaxed, on her small patio.

'You know, I wasn't sure it was you at first, you look so different from last night,' he said nonchalantly. 'And I had to guess which house it was by peering into the front windows. A process of elimination. I guessed that military prints weren't quite your style, and I couldn't imagine you curled up with a copy of *Practical Hen-Keeping* in the evening. Although, seeing you in your gardening outfit, I'm not so sure.'

She advanced towards him angrily. There was something about the sight of him in her garden, hands casually pushed down into his jeans pockets, that made her feel acutely vulnerable and threatened.

'Just tell me why you've come here and then go! I want nothing to do with you. Nothing whatsoever!'

He looked at her equably, untouched by her fury.

'You mean you're not going to offer me coffee?'

'No, I most certainly am not!'

'Well, I guess that's understandable,' he drawled. 'Did you get my flowers?'

'Yes, but if you think that makes the slightest difference to anything——'

'OK, OK!' He put up a hand as if to ward off blows. 'I didn't think they would, to tell the truth, but I felt it was the least I could do.'

She stared at him, seething, but some small part of her mind stood outside her anger, looking at him with an interest she could not help. If she looked different this morning, then so did he. He wore casual country clothes, tough brown boots and a thick navy sweater, and with his hair blowing in the wind he looked far less predatory than he had last night, in his dark formal clothes.

The way he looked at her, too, was different. His gaze seemed more open, guileless, and that brooding sensuality she had noticed at dinner was muted, although there were hints of it still in the set of his straight lips and the easy way he inhabited his body. Despite herself she found her eyes taking in the set of his shoulders, his hips in the tight worn jeans, more aware of him as a man than she found comfortable.

'What do you want?'

'Just to make my apologies in person. I behaved insufferably.' His mouth crooked. 'I blame the dress.'

'I blame you.'

'Yes,' he said, nodding slowly, as if in agreement. His eyes were searching her face. No doubt he was wondering what had happened to the woman he remembered from last night. Her face was stripped of make-up and her wellingtons were caked with mud. In her hand she grasped a muddy bundle of weeds.

'Were you drunk?' she asked abruptly. The rough intrusion of his embrace puzzled her. It seemed so at odds with the charm and sophistication he clearly had in abundance.

'If only.' He sounded almost rueful.

'What, then?'

He turned away from her question, pacing the width of her small garden. He put his hands back in his pockets and whistled through his teeth as he looked around. He was the most infuriating man she had ever met. When he made his leisurely way back to her he nodded towards the house.

'Nineteen-sixties economy model. Small rooms, large windows. Tiny kitchen. Functional bathroom. Last night I imagined you tripping up the lane to something more romantic. An eighteenth-century cottage with roses around the door, say. Or perhaps home to Mummy and Daddy at the Olde Manse, given the circles you obviously move in.'

'I don't move in any circles! And teachers' salaries don't run to eighteenth-century cottages.'

'Oh, you're a teacher! Hence the "miss".' He gave a wickedly accurate imitation of Tracey's homespun country accent. 'I did wonder.'

'You embarrassed that poor girl.'

'I did,' he acknowledged readily. 'That's another thing I don't feel too good about this morning. That was really unforgivable.'

'As opposed to all the other things which were only partly unforgivable?' she enquired sarcastically.

'I meant to kiss you.' His dark eyes flicked up to hers with a sudden deep and challenging look that made her heart dance a nervous tattoo. She wanted to look away, but she found she couldn't. 'I meant to do that from the moment I saw you walk through the drawing-room door. If it had meant flinging all the other guests aside and ravishing you on the sofa, I would have done it without a second thought. I mean——' he opened his hands in emphasis '—have you any idea what you looked like, last night! It wasn't just the dress, although heaven knows, if it was intended to turn heads it certainly did; there wasn't a man in the room who could keep his eyes off you. It was your eyes and hair and skin, the way you walked in with your head held high——' He paused for breath and she searched his face. 'Look at it from my point of view. I was prepared for the most awful stuffed-shirt country dinner party. I was already half dead from boredom, when in wafts this vision from heaven.'

'Oh, for goodness' sake!'

'All right, all right.' Again he put up a hand, grinning a little at his own hyperbole. 'But it's all true, I swear it. I meant to kiss you, come what may, and—evil little schemer that I am—I had it in mind that if I took such a liberty against your will, I would have the perfect excuse to seek you out and apologise the next day. What I didn't intend was the——' He stopped, literally lost for words.

'The violence?' she put in. 'The animal savagery?'

At last he looked discomposed. 'I really am sorry,' he said quietly and it almost looked as if there was a flush of embarrassment along his cheekbones. 'I can see that there's no reason at all why you should believe me, but I give you my word that I didn't mean to treat you—like that. I've got no excuse, but when I took you in my arms the very devil seemed to get hold of me.'

She fingered her lips and his eyes went immediately to her gesture. Her fingers touched bruised skin.

'It's a pretty speech,' she snapped, 'but if you're serious about apologising to me, the best way you can do it is to stay away from me from this moment onwards.'

'You won't let me buy you a drink?' He indicated her clothes. 'I always find gardening a thirsty business.'

'I most certainly won't!' His hide was as thick as an elephant's!

'What about some community service? Isn't that the usual punishment for first-time offenders these days? I could cart all that to the rubbish tip for you.' He indicated a mound of stones and other garden debris, the result of her morning's labour.

'I don't want you to do anything for me! I don't want you here! You don't seem to understand, I don't want anything to do with you!' She did not often lose her temper, but now her voice was rising hysterically. In some obscure way she knew he was a danger to her, and she wanted him gone.

'Come on,' he joked, 'don't beat about the bush.
Tell me what you really think!' But when he saw the
continuing hostility in her eyes his grin faded.

He's got away with too much for too long, she
thought angrily, and her heart hardened against his
considerable charms.

Their eyes locked for a moment. 'You mean there's
absolutely nothing I can do or say to you to make good
our relationship?'

'As far as I'm concerned, we have no relationship.
We never have had, and we never will have.'

He began to turn, then he swung back. 'Oh, you're
wrong there,' he said, and his eyes warmed wickedly.
'We do have a relationship.'

He paused and registered the discomposure in her
eyes. 'We're acquainted,' he went on. 'Not even you
can deny that. And when we meet—which we
undoubtedly will—if only on opposite sides of a
planning enquiry—it would be the height of rudeness
if we failed to acknowledge one another.'

'Well, you should know,' she hissed. 'When it
comes to matters of rudeness, you must be the local
expert.'

'Ow,' he said lightly. 'I think I'm going to retire and
lick my wounds. Goodbye, Sophie Walker—for the
time being.'

She stood without moving until she heard him drive
away, then she went to the end of the garden and lit a
bonfire, and spent an hour watching weeds dry and
shrivel to scraps of ash and vanish, fervently wishing
she could sear Seth Huntingdon's presence out of her
life as simply and completely.

The shrill of the telephone broke her angry trance.

'Sophie?'

'Hello, Amanda.'

'Can you talk?'

Amanda's arch tone grated on her taut nerves.

'Of course I can talk!'

'I mean, are you alone?'

'Yes, I'm gardening.'

'He's quite something, isn't he?'

'Who?'

'Who do you think?'

'I suppose you mean Seth Huntingdon,' said Sophie patiently. Every time Amanda introduced her to a new man she rang the next day to find out what Sophie thought. As a result she had perfected the art of the blandly neutral comment. But this time she could not be bothered to mask her feelings.

'Who else?' Amanda giggled suggestively. 'You must tell me, is he as—er—full of promise as he looks?'

'Amanda, what are you talking about!'

'Oh, come on, Sophie, I did introduce you, after all. I must say I was beginning to despair of ever finding a man you approved of. In fact, Tim asked me once if you were going to live like a nun for ever.'

'Well, I certainly don't approve of Seth Huntingdon!' she exploded. 'If you must know, I think he's one of the rudest, most philistine men I've ever met in my life!'

'Sophie, you don't have to pretend with me. I'm not one of your parents or school governors or anything. And the vibrations between you two were as steamy as anything last night.'

'Pretend? Amanda, maybe it's me, but we seem to be talking at cross purposes.' She rubbed her forehead, where a headache threatened.

Amanda spoke like someone throwing down a hand of aces. 'Tim drove your car round this morning. It started with no trouble. But he came straight back with it. He said Seth's Range Rover was parked outside your house, and he didn't want to embarrass you both.'

Sophie was speechless.

Amanda took her silence as an admission of guilt. 'Sophie, it's the last quarter of the twentieth century. No one thinks twice about things like this any more.'

'There aren't any "things", Amanda! I'm sorry to disappoint you, but I slept in my house last night, and I presume Seth Huntingdon slept in his!'

'You mean Tim was seeing things? That wasn't his car?'

'It was,' she said reluctantly. 'He came for something this morning. But you mustn't read anything into that. It was purely a business call.'

'Business?' she said sceptically.

'Business,' she said firmly, drawing a line under the conversation.

Amanda digested this slowly and when she spoke again there was a waspish tinge to her voice. She knew the full truth was being kept from her, and she did not like it one bit.

'Well, if that's the case, I must admit I'm disappointed, Sophie. I like to think my little schemes bear fruit now and again, and I can't help thinking a night of wild passion would do you the world of good.

If you go on like this you could end up a real old schoolmarm!'

'I can promise you I'd far rather be a shrivelled-up spinster schoolmistress than have Seth Huntingdon lay a single finger on me!' The words came out so forcefully that Amanda, with her finely tuned social antennae, immediately scented scandal.

'Goodness, what on earth's he done to you?' There was a sharp intake of breath. 'He didn't——? No, no, he wouldn't. He couldn't. He's not the type.' She paused, hopefully, but Sophie kept silent. 'Well, whatever's going on between you two, I'm sorry you feel like that about him. I must say he's one of the few men I've met of late who've made me regret I'm a respectable married woman.'

'Perhaps you should let him know how you feel. I'm sure he wouldn't let a little thing like marriage get in his way.'

'Sophie, I've never known you so bitter!'

'It's what happens to spinsters,' she said bitterly. Then she took a deep breath. 'I'm sorry, Amanda, I'm just not having a good day. It was a splendid dinner last night, and you're not responsible for the behaviour of your guests. Thank you for a lovely evening.'

'You must come again soon,' said Amanda, but her heart was not in it, and she guessed it would be some time before her name rose to the top of Amanda's carefully controlled guest-list again.

The next day Sophie telephoned Bill Fletcher, a local farmer and chairman of the Conservative Society.

'Sophie, m'dear,' he boomed down the line.

'Thought you'd given us up.'

She held the receiver away from her ear. 'No, no, not at all, Bill. But everything at school has been so haywire of late I haven't been able to get to any meetings.'

'Sorry to hear that. Trouble teaching the little blighters to read and write?' He guffawed and she had to smile.

'No, it's not the children, it's Mrs——' She stopped abruptly. It would have been nice to tap Bill's considerate wisdom of the world for her current problems, but she had a professional duty to keep silence. Gossip spread like wildfire in this quiet country area. Her heart sank as she thought that. No doubt Amanda was already busy spreading the word that something had happened between Sophie and Seth.

'Well, if there's anything I can do to help. Neil Mumford's chairman of the education committee now, up at County Hall. He's an old friend of mine.' Bill was a great believer in the 'word-in-the-ear' approach to all life's difficulties

'Thank you, Bill, but no, thanks. It will all work out. I really rang you about Sedbury Hall. Have you heard anything about what's happening to it.'

'Sedbury Hall? No, why? I know it's been sold at last. To some architect chappie, I believe.'

'Not an architect, a property developer,' she said bitterly. 'Bill, you won't believe what he wants to do.' Quickly she ran over Seth's ambitious schemes for the old manor house.

'Mmm,' said Bill slowly when she had finished. 'Can't imagine he'd be allowed to get away with that.'

'He seems to think there'll be no problem. He's quite a ruthless type, Bill. I'm sure he's used to wheeling and dealing, and he seems to have plenty of cash to throw around.'

'He'll find people down this way have independent minds. They'll soon tell him to put his cheque book away if that's his game.'

'He said the Hall was in such bad shape that no one will want it if he pulls out.'

'Hmm.' Bill paused for thought. 'He might have something there. I haven't been round the place for a few years, but even then it was on its last legs. It must be worse now.'

'I thought the Society ought to try and do something. Could you put it on the agenda for the next meeting?'

'All right, Sophie. I'll also have a word with the planning boys and find out what's what. You're a good girl to have let me know.'

Girl. She smiled a little grimly to herself as she replaced the receiver. To Bill Fletcher every woman under sixty was a girl, and at twenty-five she was probably little more than a toddler to him, despite the fact she owned her own house and held down a responsible job as head of infants at the village school.

Yet sometimes these days she felt a hundred. Her gaze strayed round her small living-room. It was warm and cosily cluttered with plants and books and papers, a Mozart quartet played softly and the coal fire flickered companionably. Yet there was little peace in her mind.

When she had fled from London back home to her native Gloucestershire this house had offered her all the solitude and security she craved. She had had a happy and contented few years here, but now all that seemed to be seeping away.

The problems at school were growing daily. She sighed. It could not go on like this, but she did not know what to do about the situation. She longed to talk it over with someone, but there was no one, either in school or outside, in whom she felt able to confide. The burden of her confusion weighed heavily on her shoulders, and she could feel her forehead frowning with the tension of her thoughts.

She stared into the fire. Maybe she should give it all up, hand in her notice, and turn her back on the problems. But she loved her job, and there were the children to think of. No, she was a teacher now, and she always would be. It was her life.

A teacher, though, or a schoolmarm, a spinster schoolmarm?

She grimaced. Amanda had hurled her barbs from spite, but there had been more truth in her words than Sophie cared to admit. She had lived alone now for so long it seemed natural to her, and she had neither needed nor wanted it otherwise. She had no boyfriends, and she never accepted dates. It had been like that ever since she had left London, it was how it had to stay, and she no longer thought to question it.

At least, she hadn't. But tonight for some reason her house seemed not quiet, but lonely, and her existence not peaceful, but sterile. There were questions surfacing in her mind that she had not dared to examine for years, and she did not have to look far to discover the reason why.

CHAPTER THREE

SOPHIE stared at Seth like a rabbit transfixed by a fox. She had hoped never to have to see him again and yet here she was, just four days later, sitting on a hard wooden chair in a bare village hall, looking at the man who had walked into her life and turned it upside down.

No, not so much upside down, she thought, as inside out, so that all her hidden feelings and desires were now on the outside, raw and hurting. When his eyes strayed to hers, as they had often done as he talked, it had been as painful as pressure on an open wound.

When Bill Fletcher had telephoned her yesterday to say that he had just heard Seth was having an open meeting in Sedbury Village Hall to 'allay fears' about his plans for the Hall, her first instinct had been to say she could not attend. But Bill had simply assumed she would be there, and so she was, even though she was exhausted and troubled by another long, difficult day at school. She told herself it was duty alone that had brought her, yet throughout the meeting her eyes had feasted hungrily on Seth's lithe, commanding figure, and followed his every word and gesture.

Now she watched him drop his hand from the planning diagrams he had been explaining, and turn to the small audience with a smile.

'And that's about it,' he concluded. 'I know some of you were worried when you heard word that part of the Hall's land was to be sold off, but I hope you can see from this that I'm not planning to break up the estate. These five acres are quite separate from the main body of land. And the houses I plan to build on them—assuming I get permission, of course—will be in the traditional style of the village——'

'Posh houses for townies!' a young farm worker interrupted angrily. 'That's what they are. Where are we supposed to live, the people who were born here? I've been saving for five years and yet I can't even afford a rabbit hutch.'

She watched Seth meet the young man's outburst with a level gaze.

'I know the sort of problems you have round here. So many people want weekend cottages in this area that prices are shooting sky-high. That's why I've included these units here.' His gesture, as he indicated the plan, was deft and descriptive. 'Two rows of traditional two-bedroomed terraced cottages. They won't be lavish, but they will be as modestly priced as I can made them.'

The farm worker said nothing, but looked mollified. Seth waited, his eyes going over the audience. Dressed in a quiet, grey suit, with a white shirt and dark tie, he looked a handsome and reassuring figure, and she could not help but notice how the women in the audience shifted on their chairs as his dark eyes lingered over them.

'Any more questions?'

His eyes roved over the hall again, coming finally to rest on Sophie's grey gaze. As he did so, a wriggle of

sensation wormed through her and she had an almost
irresistible urge to uncross and recross her legs, to
mask how she felt. But instead she jumped to her feet.

'Yes. This is all very well, but what about the Hall?
You've hardly said a word about what you intend to
do with that!'

Seth's eyes darkened as he looked at her.

'I think I said there was a major restoration job to be
done there. The fabric of the building has been
allowed to decay so far that almost every part of it
needs treatment.'

'Then what?' she said bluntly.

He stepped towards where she stood, and his eyes
glittered. 'I have to say my plans, at this stage, are
entirely—fluid.'

'Fluid? What does that mean?' Her curls stirred
around her shoulders as she shook her head angrily.
'People here are worried about the future of the Hall.
You don't seem to realise.'

'I realise that very well,' he snapped back. 'Why else
do you think I am here? I don't have to hold a meeting
like this. I simply felt it would be a friendly
community gesture.'

'A friendly community whitewash, you mean!' Her
voice rose to a background of muttering in the hall.

Seth held her eyes. 'I've said I'm going to restore
the Hall. Beyond that, at this stage, I can't say.'

'Can't or won't?'

'Can't.' He echoed, and his voice was clipped. 'I
can't because I don't know.'

'I thought you knew only too well, right down to
the fax machines in the library!'

The muttering increased in volume. Seth shifted his

gaze from her to the rest of his audience, and smiled as if to enlist their sympathy.

'What Miss Walker is talking about here is some musings I shared with her when we happened to meet socially last week. It was merely idle party conversation, nothing more. I didn't for a moment expect her to take every word I said literally. In fact, I'm afraid I was guilty of teasing her a little.'

A ripple of sympathetic laughter spread through the hall. Encouraged he added with a grin, 'I probably wouldn't have dared to be quite so flippant if I had realised at the time that she is an esteemed local schoolmistress.' The laughter he drew was warm and friendly, but she only heard jeers and mockery.

'Oh!' She drew her breath in sharply and colour flushed to her cheeks.

He turned and let her eyes linger long on her blushing, angry face, before turning back to the audience.

'Restoration of the Hall,' he continued smoothly, 'will be enormously expensive. That is why I am building the new houses I have just told you about. Despite local rumours to the contrary, I don't have that sort of cash in my bank, and the new houses will, I hope, subsidise the bulk of the work on the Hall. After that, I shall have to see how things work out. It could be a magnificent family home,' his eyes slid back to hers, then away again, 'but it might have to earn its keep as a hotel, or a conference centre. As I said, it all depends——'

'Oh what?' Sophie challenged him again, her eyes deepening to a violet grey anger. 'Surely we're at least entitled to know that!'

His eyes went to hers like dark, probing lasers, and his mouth was set in a firm line. 'It depends,' he said slowly, and his eyes continued to scour her face until she found she was gripping the back of the chair in front to prevent herself from shaking, 'on the future. And since neither you, nor I, nor anyone in this hall tonight has the faintest idea what that holds for us, we'll just have to wait and see.'

His eyes held hers for another long moment, as if their conversation were private, and the other twenty people in the room did not exist, then snapped away.

He ran a hand through his hair. 'Any more questions? Or if there are, perhaps you'd prefer to put them to me in the Sedbury Arms, which is where you'll find me for the next half-hour or so, attached to a pint of best bitter.' He turned and began to put papers back in his brief case, and the hall slowly emptied of people.

Sophie reached for her handbag on the floor beside her and found as she gripped the worn leather strap that her hands were still shaking.

'Never mind, love. You did your best to pin him down.' Bill Fletcher put a consoling hand on her arm. 'You all right to get home? Only I've got to rush. I told Grace I'd be home by ten for once.'

She gave him a bleak nod and turned to leave.

'Sophie.'

She stopped, not turning.

'Sophie, wait.'

Slowly she turned to face him. Anger and humiliation still churned within her. 'What is it?'

Seth began to speak but as he did so a last straggler from the audience went up to him and caught at his sleeve.

'That was a good show, Mr Huntingdon. I'll buy
you a pint for your trouble.' Seth smiled quickly at the
older man. 'Thanks, I'll be over in a few minutes.
Sophie,' he said again, as the man walked out.

'I'm waiting,' she said, through gritted teeth.

'I'll buy you a drink.'

'What?' she exploded with fury. 'You must be
joking. After the way you just humiliated me in front
of all those people——'

'Don't be ridiculous! Nobody thought you were
humiliated. Anyway, you deserved it. You shouldn't
have taken what I said so seriously.'

'Perhaps I wouldn't have, if you'd come up with
any plausible alternative tonight. But you didn't, did
you! It was all just fine words and gestures, but not a
whisper about what you're really going to do with the
Hall.'

'For heaven's sake, how many times do you have to
be told. It's because I don't know myself at this stage!'

'I don't believe you!' she flung back. 'It made me
sick, watching you up there pretending to be Mr
Nice, telling everyone how thoughtful you were
because you've decided to build them some dinky
little terraced houses. Prattling on about consultation
and negotiation and all that stuff when no doubt
you've already got the contractors lined up and ready
to start digging the foundations.'

'If there had been any serious objections tonight I
would have had to take them into account,' he said
swiftly, 'but otherwise I have to move fast.'

'You see! When do they start? Is it tomorrow, or the
day after?'

'Sophie, stop it,' he said, and he suddenly sounded weary. 'You know I have to operate within the normal planning procedures, just like anyone else.'

'Oh, yes? I thought you said money always talked.' She hardly recognised her own voice, it sounded so hard and nasty.

'I seem to have said a lot of things the other night. I didn't expect to have every one of them taken down and used in evidence against me!'

'Perhaps you should learn to be a bit more careful with your words—not to mention your actions.' She was so tired and stressed, she spoke without thinking.

He thumped his fist down angrily on his briefcase. 'How many times do you want me to say sorry for what I did to you? Do I have to crawl across the floor and abase myself at your feet?'

'All I want you to do is to come clean about your intentions. I've been involved in lots of planning fights round here, and if there's one thing I've learned it's that property developers always know what their plans are, even when they pretend they don't. Or are you now going to deny you're even a property developer?'

His eyes narrowed. 'Since you mention it, perhaps I might. But as I'm clearly in the business of building houses, then clearly I must be a property developer. There wouldn't be much point in denying it, would there?'

'There, then.'

'Where, then? What's so terrible about what? I can see that in your book it's probably better to have no new houses, no new factories, no new shopping-centres—just lots of picture-postcard villages full of picture-postcard cottages. But life isn't like that. People have to work, live. After all, you wouldn't have a roof over your head if someone twenty years ago hadn't decided to buy up a piece of land on the edge of Bicknor and build four houses on it.'

'That was just some disused Army wasteland! We're talking about one of the most beautiful houses in the county.'

'Beautiful and derelict! Have you been inside it lately? There's hardly a floorboard that you don't go straight through when you tread on it. Another couple of years and the whole lot would have had to be pulled down. Anything I do with it has to be better than that!'

'No, it wouldn't, not if you go ahead with your all-weather domes and whatever.'

His teeth were gritted with exasperated fury. 'Haven't I made myself clear? That was just dinner-table talk.'

'That's what you say! But why should I trust you? You just say what you want, do what you want—and if anyone tries to stop you, you brush them aside as if they're no more important than ants.' To her horror, tears of anger and frustration threatened to close her throat.

'Then just what the hell am I doing here!' he shouted, and his held-in anger finally broke over her like a cold torrent. 'If I don't care about anybody or anything, just tell me, Sophie Walker, why I am wasting my time in this dreary village hall, wasting my breath talking to people who prefer rumour to fact, wasting my emotions trying to prove to you that I'm not the evil ogre you seem to want me to be!'

'I'll tell you why! I'll tell you exactly why!' His fury made tears tremble in her eyes, but she held herself on a tight rein, only her breath coming in ragged sobs of fury. 'It's easy. Because it suits your purposes to do so. Because you think you'll get an easier ride if you pretend to tell people what you're doing to their village! Because you think that that charming smile of yours, and those reassuring words, will get you anywhere you want. It's just politics. The politics of the predator!'

His face darkened at her words, and his expression made her catch her breath.

'Oh, that's it, is it?' In a second he had strode over to her and was gripping both her wrists in a grasp so tight it hurt. His eyes were harsh and bitter, only inches from hers. She could see a pulse beating at his neck and smell the scent of anger on his skin, and his voice when it came was hoarse and dangerous. 'Well, maybe you're right. With those huge doe eyes of yours and that infuriating righteous anger, you certainly make me feel predatory, angry and predatory.' His eyes raked hers and his lips parted, showing a gleam of teeth.

'Stop it!'

She stepped back, pulling from his grip, but as she did so, she stumbled against a chair, dragging him with her. For a second, his body was pressed against hers, length to length, and the shock of it, lean and hard, sent an instant answering flare of desire through her.

'Only it doesn't, does it? It doesn't get me anywhere I want?' he continued mercilessly, steadying himself with a hand on another chair and pulling himself away from her so that he could read her eyes and the trembling of her lips. 'Because you know, and I know, where that is—but since you so clearly loathe the very ground I step on, I can't imagine that there is anything I could ever do to make that particular desire come to fruition.'

She swallowed hard and rubbed at her wrists. She could not bear to meet his eyes, but looked down to the bare, dusty floor, battling with the blush that threatened to heat her face, and the tears in her eyes. She was exhausted, desolate, vulnerable. Yet the last thing in the world she wanted was to show him either tears or embarrassment.

'I don't know what you're talking about,' she said tightly. 'I'm talking about houses. About Sedbury Hall. All I want to know is what you're going to do with it.'

He put out a hand and tipped her chin up, not gently but with the roughness of barely controlled anger.

'Of course you know what I'm talking about. Don't pretend the village innocent with me, Sophie, because I can see in your eyes that you know more of the world than that. And as for Sedbury Hall, as I seem to have said before tonight, that will depend on factors outside my control. But when I know the answer, I'll try and remember to let you know.'

CHAPTER FOUR

'GOOD morning, Sophie.'

'Good morning, Mrs Werner. Isn't it a terrible morning?'

It was a cold and bleak start to the week. All hints of spring had vanished beneath a leaden blanket of rain and children arriving early at the school were not lingering in the playground but hurrying into the steamy cloakrooms. The headmistress, however, stood in the downpour without a hat or umbrella, seemingly oblivious to the elements.

'It's not like you to be late, Sophie.'

'I'm not late, Mrs Werner. Look, it's only twenty to nine.' She showed her her watch.

'Oh, yes,' said the head vaguely, 'I thought—I seem to have been here a long time.'

'Perhaps your watch is fast,' Sophie suggested, soothingly, and began to lead the older woman gently into the building. But inwardly she sighed at the thought of the week ahead. Images of Seth had filled her head for days, and left her sleepless at nights. She felt restless and unrefreshed by her troubled weekend. Now it was Monday, she had not yet reached the school door, yet her problems had already begun.

'You're awfully wet,' she said. 'Wouldn't you like to pop home and change and get an umbrella? I'll take assembly.' She held her breath. Sometimes the headmistress went along happily with her suggestions, but at other times her old authority returned and she fiercely resisted any attempts to direct her. Please go home, she prayed silently, not wanting the children to see their headmistress standing up in front of them so wet and bedraggled.

'Yes, perhaps I'll do that.' Mrs Werner nodded, and Sophie let out her breath in relief, and turned to begin the day's work.

It wasn't easy. First there was a hasty assembly to prepare. Then there was the usual string of problems that heralded the start of every week. A radiator was leaking in the cloakroom, and one of the class teachers telephoned in to say her car had broken down and she would not be in until late.

She dealt quickly and efficiently with all the matters in hand, ruthlessly driving away all thoughts of Seth's disturbing dark eyes. Over the past term, as Mrs Werner's mental health had slowly waned, Sophie had grown used to assuming responsibility for the school. In fact her life was a hundred times easier when the head was off the premises, since Mrs Werner's decisions and actions had become increasingly unpredictable.

Even so, the strain was beginning to tell on her. For a moment, sitting behind Mrs Werner's chaotic desk, she felt as if she had barely the strength to get through the day, let alone the week, or the rest of the term. But then she walked into the school hall, and the children's familiar, eager faces gave her the injection of new energy she so badly needed.

She smiled. 'Good morning, everybody. There are quite a few notices this morning, but shall we first sing "All Things Bright and Beautiful"?'

The assembly went well and the children filed quietly off to their classrooms. She settled her own group of five-year-olds down with one of the parents who had come in to help, then hurried back to the head's office to see if Mrs Werner had returned.

A tall, dark-suited man was standing outside and her heart suddenly leapt up and clamoured behind her ribs, but when he turned he was an unknown middle-aged man. She struggled to calm herself, hating Seth for the state he had got her into.

'Can I help you? I'm Sophie Walker, the head of the lower school.'

'Ah, yes, Miss Walker. My name's Raynor, George Raynor. Education Department, County Hall.'

'Oh!' She could not hide her surprise. Unknown official visitors were rare at this quiet village school.

'Mrs Werner's expecting me.'

'She is? I mean, I'm sure she is. I'll just see——' She opened the door and checked the empty office. Sometimes when Mrs Werner 'popped' home she did not come back all day.

'I'm sure she'll be back in a moment. Would you like to take a seat.'

'Thank you.' The man sat down and took a sheaf of papers from his briefcase. 'I'm here to finalise the arrangements for the inspection,' he informed her.

'Inspection?'

The man frowned. 'The inspection. By Her Majesty's Inspectors. One of their routine school checks, that's all. Nothing to worry about. Although most schools go into a flat spin when they hear about it, painting the loos and polishing the computers.

Surely your head's told you all.'

She shook her head dumbly. 'It must have slipped her mind.'

The man raised her eyebrows. 'Well, I have to admire the lady's confidence. Perhaps she's sure there's nothing to worry about, nothing to sweep away under the carpet—not that most school budgets stretch to carpets!' He laughed heavily and Sophie smiled with stiff facial muscles.

'If you'll excuse me, I will see if I can find her for you.'

She stood in the corridor, frozen with panic, her mind racing. Then she decided to take a chance. If Mrs Werner suddenly reappeared it would be a disaster, but the chances were she would not. Quickly she went to the cloakroom and checked her appearance. As usual, in working-hours, she looked coolly competent in a black trousers and a blue silk shirt. She combed her hair and put on some lipstick before making her way back to Mr Raynor.

Sitting down behind the desk she regarded him firmly. 'I'm sorry, I've only just been told this, but Mrs Werner was taken ill this morning. A sudden gastric attack,' she improvised. 'She had to go home after assembly and she's unlikely to be back. Would you mind going over things with me? I am in charge when the head is absent.'

'Not at all, not at all. There's very little to it, just a question of confirming all this is convenient for the school.' He fanned out a bemusing array of papers on the desk. 'It will be the usual sort of team. Four and a leader. They'll arrive on Monday.'

'Monday,' she echoed faintly.

'Monday. Next Monday at nine o'clock. They'll be in school for a week looking at all aspects of the curriculum, buildings, resources, school meals and so on. They will observe lessons, but teachers are instructed to make no special efforts, only carry on as normal.' The man's voice eased into a soporific bureaucratic hum. When he finished she took a breath.

'That all seems in order. But what happens if Mrs Werner is still ill? She hasn't been in the best of health lately. Would the inspection still go ahead.'

'HMI work on a tight schedule,' he said pompously. 'If they cancelled their plans for every dose of flu, they would soon be in a pretty pickle.'

'I see.'

Mr Raynor stood up. 'I'm sure you're busy, with your head away. I'll show myself out.' He shook her head. 'Thank you for your time.'

'Goodbye.'

'Goodbye.'

The rest of the day passed in a blur. Sophie's thoughts were in such turmoil that she could barely concentrate on her teaching. The rain did not cease and the children, cooped up all day, grew irritable and noisy. At last the final bell went and peace slowly settled on the building as the last stragglers left for home.

She went back to Mrs Werner's office and without ceremony began to rifle through the filing-cabinet. Things were in an impossible muddle, and dusk was drawing in before she found the papers she was looking for, folded and torn, at the bottom of a file.

She switched on the desk light and read through

them methodically, smoothing and ordering the pages
as she tried to smooth and order her thoughts. But she
was so tired that after a time the print jumped and
juggled before her eyes.

'Oh.' She groaned. Then she thrust her fingers
under her hair and closed her eyes and immediately a
dark figure loomed up to haunt her thoughts.

'Burning the midnight oil?' said a dark, teasing voice.
'I didn't think teachers did that. Everyone knows they
only do the job for the short hours and long holidays.'

It was as if a phantom had spoken. Her eyes flew
open, but the desk light blurred her vision so all she
could see was a dark shape in the doorway.

'I don't know what you're doing here,' she said
tiredly, 'but if you've come to talk to me, I'd like you
to go away.'

He walked forward. 'Chocolates,' he said,
proffering one hand. 'Champagne.' He proffered the
other. 'You see, I'm still trying to find an acceptable
way to make amends.'

'What for?' Her voice sounded flat. She had ached
to see him, but now she felt too weary for the
emotional turmoil that seemed to follow in his wake.

He shrugged. 'Everything—molesting you, shouting at you, losing my temper with you. I can't seem to
keep a decent hold on myself when you're in the
vicinity. Although I have to say you gave me quite a
lot of provocation the other night.'

'I have never felt less in the mood for chocolates or
champagne,' she said with slow, defeated deliberation.

'No,' he said, and put his offerings quietly on the
desk. She felt his eyes go over her face. 'No. I can see

that. I waited outside your house hoping to catch you.
Then when I drove past the school, I saw there were
still lights on. I hope you don't mind me coming in.'

'What do you want?' She was talking to a shape in
the darkness. It was an unreal end to an unreal day.

'Just to say sorry. Really and truly, Sophie. I've
behaved abominably towards you, one way and
another. I don't know what gets into me.'

'It doesn't matter. It all seems a million years ago
now.'

He sat on the edge of the desk. 'What is it?' His
voice was gentle.

She shook her head.

'It often helps to talk things through.'

'It's—too complicated.'

'I'm not stupid,' he coaxed. He smiled. 'I'll even
show you my qualifications some time, to prove it.'

Her eyes went over the muddled desk, the tottering
piles of papers balanced on chairs. 'Oh.' Panic rose up
in her chest, and to her horror tears started in her eyes
and one ran down her cheek. She dashed it away, but
suddenly sobs were choking her and her whole body
shook as all the tensions of the day, and all the days
that had gone before, were racking her through.

'Hey.' He stood up and came round the desk and
took her shoulders while she cried. His hands were
firm but light, as if he were frightened to hold her too
closely, yet the very thoughtfulness of his touch
released more tears.

'Tell me a little, at any rate. Don't sit here in the
dark getting in a state.'

'I wouldn't know where to start.'

'At the beginning?'

'That's a long time ago. My problems are more immediate.'

'If you define the problem, you often find you're describing the solution.'

'If only it were that easy,' she said bitterly. She wiped her tears, pushing her chair back from the light into welcoming darkness. When she looked at Seth she could see the shadow of his profile and the hard line of his thigh along the desk, but little more. She wanted to put out a hand and touch his strength. 'Management jargon isn't all that helpful in these particular circumstances.'

'Perhaps it's worth a try. What's your most pressing problem?'

'The school inspectors. They're coming down from London next week.'

'And?'

'And! You see, you don't understand! To us, they're like God. We're going to have a full inspection. Five of them putting us under a microscope for a week.'

'So, is there something wrong with the school?'

'There's something wrong with every school. And the inspectors always find it.'

'And what will they find here?'

She answered promptly. 'We aren't as strong as we could be on maths or music. And if I were in charge, I would want a better system for picking up the learning difficulties some children have.'

'But you aren't in charge, are you? So why are you sitting here in the dark agonising about it all? It's not your responsibility.'

She hesitated, torn by loyalty and distress. But she had carried her worries around for so long that she

longed to confide them to someone. She could not talk
to the other teachers, or parents, or anyone in the
village. But if anyone was an outsider, surely Seth
was? He was new to the area and knew none of the
people concerned. And the burden of her problems
was like a weight pressing her down in her chair.

'Someone has to be in charge,' she said slowly, 'and
that someone is me. I'm Mrs Werner's deputy.'

'She's the headmistress?'

'On paper, but—oh, Seth, it's awful. She's been
quite vague for a term or two now, but just lately she's
become much worse. Sometimes she seems quite
batty. This morning she didn't even know what time
it was. And she told me off for being late, even though
I was early. She was standing in the playground
getting soaked, but she didn't even seem to notice.
Then when I sent her home to get changed she
vanished for the rest of the day.'

'Haven't other people noticed? What about the
parents, or the staff?'

'The teachers realise, of course, but they don't
know quite how bad she is. Even I didn't realise quite
how terrible things had become until today. Until
tonight, really, when I had a chance to look round
here.' With her arm she gesticulated at the muddled
papers. 'I've been covering up a lot for her, too.
Making sure the school keeps going.'

'And that's taken its toll,' he said shrewdly.

She nodded, wearily. 'I've tried not to let my own
teaching suffer, but sometimes I feel as if I'm doing
the work of ten people.'

'You can't go on like this. If you do you'll crack up
as well, and where will that leave the school?'

'I know.' She closed the file in front of her and looked up at his shadowed face. 'I've known it for a long time, really, but today finally brought it home.'

There was silence in the little room. She could sense his mind turning. After a moment he said, 'Your first problem is to get through next week. Do you want the inspectors to know how things really are, or not?'

She, too, thought carefully before she answered. 'They're bound to see some of the problems. They're too experienced to be hoodwinked completely. But if they see the full story, they'll talk to County Hall and insist she be forcibly retired.'

'Wouldn't that be the best thing?'

'No, no, it wouldn't.' Talking to him she found her thoughts falling clearly into place. 'She has to retire, I can see that now, but the best thing would be if she made up her mind for herself. Then she could go with dignity and honour, and she deserves that. She's devoted herself to the school for years, and she was a fine headmistress in her day. She can't help what is happening to her now.'

'So what are you going to do?'

'I think I might be able to persuade her to stay out of school for that week. She's obviously frightened about the inspection—all the papers about it have been pushed to the bottom of the filing-cabinet and she hasn't told any of the staff about it. She might be only too pleased to let me take over.

'If I work hard this week I can put a lot of things in order, and what can't be covered up—well, it won't hurt for the inspectors to see that some things have been let slip by a head teetering on the verge of retirement.'

'And is she?'

She sighed heavily. 'No, but I'm going to have to persuade her. That's the really difficult bit.'

'One step at a time, Sophie. You've got enough on your plate for the next fortnight.'

She looked up at him, her eyes large and dark in the low light. 'Yes, but I feel better now. At least I know what I've got to try and do. Although whether I'll be able to——' She shook her head.

'I'm sure you will.'

He spoke so certainly that her eyes widened.

'Do you really think so?'

'Yes. I do.' He got up. 'But not tonight. You're exhausted. Get your coat and I'll drive you home.'

Outside her house he nodded at the darkened windows and said, 'If you like I'll come in and make you coffee and scramble you some eggs. You're all-in.'

The thought startled her with warmth and longing. No one had done anything like that for her for years. Her house was always dark when she came home, and she was often too tired to cook. How wonderful it would be to be loved and looked after like that. She glanced across to him, surprised by his offer, and in the darkness she saw him grin and the gleam of his teeth threw all her defences back on guard.

This was no kind and caring friend, but Seth Huntingdon, the hungry wolf who had assaulted her so unceremoniously the other night. If she let him into her house, he would certainly eat her up!

As if to confirm her worst suspicions he added, 'I'll even put a hot-water bottle in your bed for you.'

'No, thank you. I'll see to my own hot-water bottles!' Her hand was on the door handle. 'Thank you for listening to me—it helped.'

'My pleasure.' His smile faded and his eyes searched hers. 'I suppose I'm wasting my time asking to see you again.'

'I'm going to be very busy.' For some reason her throat was dry. She swallowed. 'You know how much I've got on my plate.'

'For the next fortnight. But after that? And I'd like to know what happens.'

She hesitated.

'I'll call you,' he said firmly.

She met his look, smoke-blue wary eyes on dark, insistent ones.

'You won't put the phone down on me?' She could feel the force of his will, bending hers.

'No,' she slowly, 'no, I won't do that.'

'Good,' he said. 'I'll consider that a promise.'

CHAPTER FIVE

BUT Seth did not ring. For two weeks Sophie had barely thought of him. Pressing problems had crowded in on her and filled her every waking moment. She had taught and lobbied and cajoled and organised, and the whole of the last five days had been filled with the relentless strain of the inspectors' visit.

Yet now she paced her house restlessly, wound up like a spring, glowering from time to time at the stubbornly silent phone.

Somewhere, deep down, she had expected him to contact her just as soon as she was free again. She had carried in her subconscious the notion he was thinking of her throughout the past two hellish weeks, and that thought had given her the strength she had needed to battle through.

But she had been at home for more than two hours now, and the house had been as silent as a grave.

'Oh!' She needed an outlet for the coiled tension inside her, but there was no one she wanted to call, nowhere she wanted to go. She went upstairs and ran the deepest, hottest bath she could bear, lavishly pouring in perfumed bath oil, but the embrace of the silky water gave her no release. When she lay back and closed her eyes her overworked brain saw only a fevered, fragmented movie of the past few days.

She got out, damp and flushed, and wrapped her white satin robe around her. There was no point in getting dressed again. She wasn't going anywhere tonight.

In the kitchen she opened the fridge and her eye fell on the unopened bottle of champagne Seth had pressed on her when he had found her at school that night. Well, why not? She had something to celebrate, after all. She took it out and reached for a glass, and at that moment the doorbell rang.

'I see you're expecting me.' Seth smiled at her, nodding at the bottle in her hand as he walked confidently past her into the living-room. 'Olives. Smoked salmon. Prawn and avocado salad. Bread. Butter. Bottle of Sancerre.' He unloaded packages on to her table. 'Oh, and a wicked chocolate gateau for pud.'

'I thought you would telephone.'

'I took a chance and just came round. Are you going to throw me out? I'll go quietly, if you've got other plans.'

She looked at him, tall, dark-haired and impossibly handsome, a powerful presence in her tiny house. He wore dark trousers and a white shirt, with an expensive but battered tweed jacket that emphasised the broad litheness of his build.

'I've got no plans,' she admitted. Her heart was bumping in her chest.

'Good. We can have a picnic. And a——' his eyes roamed hers, reading for clues '—celebratory drink?' he finished, tentatively.

'A well-earned one, at least. You've caught me by surprise. I'll go and change.'

His hand shot out and took her wrist. 'Don't. You look lovely as you are, and about five times as decent as you did in your skimpy dinner dress when we first met. And anyway, I want to hear how it all went. Here.'

She yielded up the bottle to his commanding hand and went to fetch plates and cutlery, her thoughts whirling. She had imagined talking to him, on the telephone, distantly, not in this sudden burst of domestic intimacy.

Yet she could not help being glad he was here, and she watched him covertly from the kitchen as he roamed her room, switching a lamp on here, turning a light off there, and selecting a cassette for her tape-deck. He looked at the fireplace, and called through, 'Can I light this?' and, seeing her nod, bent quickly to the task. In what seemed like only moments he had transformed her room into a glowing haven, lit by low lamps and warmed by crackling flames, and somehow inhabited it in a way she had never fully done when she was alone.

'Glasses, Sophie. Quickly.' He opened the champagne expertly, careful to avoid any amateurish cascade of bubbles, and poured deftly.

'To you. To your evident survival.' His eyes warmed at her over his glass and set her heart beating faster. She drank quickly, 'Come and sit down and tell me what happened.'

He drew her to the sofa. She drank again and felt the sparkling liquid slip down to release the pent-up tension inside her.

'It's hard to remember exactly what happened now. I thought the worst bit would be trying to persuade

Mrs Werner to stay away from the school, but that was relatively easy. When she came back to school and I had to remind her about the visit she actually blanched.' She began her tale slowly but soon the words were coming easily. 'I've read about people doing that in novels, but it was weird seeing it. All the colour drained from her face, and she swayed backwards as if someone had tried to hit her.

'I offered to stay after school and help her get things in order and she jumped at it. Then, during the week, she got twitchier and twitchier, and when I suggested she was ill and should go home to bed, she hardly bothered to argue. The rest of the staff were marvellous.'

'Did you tell them the truth?'

'No, I just said she was ill and wouldn't be around for a week or so, but it was a conspiracy of silence. Everyone knew what that really meant. The inspectors seemed a bit put out at first, but then they just got on with their job.'

'And that went all right?' His eyes were on hers, dark and warm. It was extraordinary, she thought, but he really seemed interested. His gaze seemed to draw the words from her in a tumble of thoughts and impressions.

'I think so. At least, it went as well as it could under the circumstances. Although can you imagine what it's like trying to do your job for a week with someone perched on a stool in the corner making notes on everything you do?'

He shook his head, smiling. 'I wouldn't stand for it.'

'You'd have to, if you were a teacher. It's absolute hell at first. You drop things and stumble over your words, and the children keep giggling. But after a time you just have to forget he's there and get on as best you can.' She thought back over the week. 'The chief inspector—he was a nice man, I liked him a lot—gave me a briefing on what the team was likely to say in their report. He made it clear they would emphasise that the school appeared to lack leadership, although he said they had been impressed by the standards that had been maintained in spite of this.'

'What about the maths, and those other things you were worrying about?'

'Oh, they picked up on all of those. I would have been surprised if they hadn't. It's perfectly clear what the school needs.'

'Clear to you. Maybe they'll make you the head, when the post comes free.'

For a moment her eyes glowed at the thought of the challenge, and she drank again, reflectively, from a glass that had been refilled without her noticing, then she shook her head at the absurdity until her hair gleamed like palest honey in the lamplight. 'They wouldn't look twice at me. I'm too young, and I haven't got enough experience.'

'How much experience have you got? You know, I don't know the first thing about you.'

'Not enough. I trained in London and stayed on to teach there for two years. I really enjoyed it. The children were tough, but they were sparky. I would have been happy to stay on there but——' She broke off abruptly and her face paled as the ghosts of her past stirred restlessly. He waited and she felt his eyes scrutinise her face too closely for comfort. 'I knew I was a country girl at heart,' she went on quickly, 'so I got a job at a school near here and came home to Gloucestershire. I only moved to my present job a year ago. So, you see,' she finished, 'with less than five years in the job, I don't rate my promotion chances that highly.'

He looked at her for a long time. 'They'd be mad to pass the opportunity by,' he said at last, 'but that's the trouble with bureaucracies. They'd always rather do the safe thing than the right one.'

For a moment she remembered Sedbury Hall, Seth's joking plans for jacuzzis and a plastic all-weather dome. There would be no bureaucracies there. But she pushed the thought quickly away. She was happy, quite incredibly happy, and she didn't want anything to spoil the moment, least of all any thoughts of Seth's true nature.

As if seeing the various shadows that had fallen across her face, Seth said, 'Let's eat. Stay there and relax. I'll bring everything over.'

She obeyed his command, following him with her eyes as he moved around the room. All his movements were swift and deft, she thought, and she took pleasure in watching how he bent and moved and how his competent, fascinating hands laid out the feast on the rug before the fire. She felt amazing. The champagne had gone to her head, but in the nicest possible way, so that the room seemed to pulse gently and when she tried to follow a train of thought it danced away from her in a rainbow fragment of images.

She put down her glass and stretched her arms high against the cushions.

'The champagne's gone to my head.'

He looked up at her, at the white satin stretched tight over her full breasts. 'Good.'

Something trembled momentarily inside her as she saw where his eyes went.

Then he grinned, very slightly. 'You don't need to look like that. I only meant good, you needed to relax. Although,' he added deliberately, 'I suppose I deserve your wariness. After all, I've never hidden my evil intentions.'

His eyes held hers and would not let them go, and the brooding sensuality she had first seen in him returned to his lips, to the darkness of his look, as he took in the sight of her. She guessed what his thoughts were and felt frightened and excited, suddenly driven by a need to loosen her tight rein on life. Her blood pounded.

'Yes,' she said very slowly, her thoughts turning inside her head, and he nodded silently when he heard her, as if something unspoken was agreed between them.

When she looked back over the evening later, with all the chilling clarity of hindsight, she could see that that had been the moment when everything had changed, but at the time, she registered only a fizz through her body as if the very blood in her veins had changed to champagne.

Naturally, picnicking on the floor as they were, it seemed sensible that she should move down to sit next to him on the rug, and since it was hot down there by the fire Seth removed his jacket to eat. Then, as they ate, sitting side by side with their backs against the sofa, it seemed quite natural that he should feed her choice titbits from his plate, and she should turn, laughing, to him and suddenly notice the fall of dark hair at his neck or the brown muscles of his throat.

They talked easily, about anything that came into their heads, although afterwards she would have been hard pressed to relate any details of their conversation, interspersed as it was by appreciative murmurs about the taste of the smoked salmon and the crisp bite of the wine.

'Pudding?' He indicated the chocolate cake.

'I'm too full.'

'Maybe later.'

She yawned. It had been such a long day, and sleep was stealing up on her. She gazed into the fire and thought about nothing at all and somehow her head was dropping to his shoulder and his arm was going about her shoulders to cradle her to him.

For a long time neither of them spoke, then Seth said in a low, rough voice, 'Sophie?'

She turned and saw the almost cruel sensuality of his look, so close to her eyes. As if coming to her senses she inhaled the warm musky smell of him, and felt the pressure of his fingers on her arm, and started to pull back. This wasn't meant to be happening.

But it was. No sooner had the thought taken shape than Seth had confirmed it with his lips. They came down on hers softly, yearningly, in a kiss so utterly different from the crazed force of his first embrace that they instantly banished all reason. A keen, swift ache went through her as he explored her mouth, taking her lips slowly at first, tentatively and gently, but hardening as he realised she was not resisting him.

Just the opposite, in fact. Coming on top of the delights of the evening, the tempting wine and food,

the unutterable luxury of being able to unburden
herself freely of her problems, and the slow, luxurious
unwinding from all her tensions, she instinctively
moved in his arms to yield up her face for more of the
glorious sensations he was conjuring inside her.

Her mouth opened to his and his tongue explored
its softness, on and on, until she could have fainted
with the delight of it.

Then he stopped, resting his forehead against her
shoulder to gain his composure before getting lightly
to his feet.

She blinked, like an owl in daylight, wondering
what to do or say.

'Shall I make some coffee?' she said awkwardly.

'Thank you, that would be nice.' He had turned
away from her and was beginning to inspect her
collection of cassettes, as suddenly formal and
uncertain as she felt. In the kitchen she fumbled,
dropped spoons. Think, think, said her brain, but she
could not, would not. Nothing seemed quite real any
more. Only Seth, and his eyes and arms and lips.

She went back out, holding two cups. The music on
the tape deck was low, moody jazz. He looked at her
standing in the doorway in her satin robe and came
across and took the cups from her and set them on the
table.

She said nothing, only looked at him with enormous
eyes.

'Come here.'

He turned her easily in his arms and began to move
with her to the music, a sensuous, slow dance in
which their feet barely moved but the music seemed
to flow through them like honey.

'Sophie Walker, you do terrible things to me. I haven't been able to think straight for weeks.' His voice was an intimate rough whisper against her ear, making her neck shiver with delight.

She swallowed.

'I was going to leave—but I can't. I have to kiss you again,' he said and he did, with his hands sliding up over her shoulders and into her hair to cup the shape of her head as he kissed her long and arousingly. Their bodies were length to length, chest, hip and thigh, each tightening to the needs of the other.

She heard him taking breath, a tortured sigh as if the kiss gave him pain. She understood that pain, that need. From a distance she heard a stifled moan that could only have come from herself.

Now he was taking her lips again and setting every atom of her being trembling. She had not felt like this for years, if ever before. She had lived quietly, her celibacy unbreached even by a casual kiss, and she had always intended that that was how things would stay.

Her physical needs had died, she had thought, back in London, all those years ago when she had loved and lost everything, her lover and in some dark way herself, and since then her solo lifestyle had never caused her the slightest concern.

But now she could see those needs had not died at all, merely been penned back behind a dam—a dam that was now threatened by the bursting pressure of Seth's attentions.

'Oh, Sophie, oh!' He spoke even as he kissed her, his lips moving against hers. Now he was kissing her harder and deeper and his hands moved down to open the throat of her robe and mould the full flesh beneath.

She threw back her head and he kissed the soft skin of her throat, and she groaned at the feeling of his caress. How could she ever have thought she could be celibate? She needed his loving more than she needed anything in the whole wide world.

Then his hands were on her back, knowing the curves of her hips, holding her tighter against him so that she knew that his needs were as great as hers, and her hands were roaming his shoulders, desperate to know the warmth of bare skin.

And somewhere in all this was the music, a sweet yearning saxophone melody that wound its way through their tightening embrace urging them towards release.

'Sophie?'

'Yes?'

They were barely speaking, but groaning against each other's mouths.

'You know what.'

'Yes.'

'Come.' He was leading her to the stairs. Yes. She had meant yes, she knew what he was asking. Not yes, yes. Or had she? She didn't know, and it was too late to sort it out because he was leading her unerringly towards her bedroom as if he knew every door in her house.

Then he gave her no time for doubts. He was a sensuous man, who knew how to take and give pleasure. By the bed he kissed her again, and ran one hand down the length of her hip and thigh, then back again, under the silky material, over the taut slimness of her figure. He cupped her hipbone.

'Nothing?' He murmured as he felt the long line of her bare skin unbroken by any hint of silk or lace, and there was the warmth of humour as well as ardour in his voice. 'Heaven forgive me, but I've wondered about that all evening.' If it had been light enough to see him she knew he would have one of his expressive eyebrows raised in self-mockery. But the only light in the room came from the landing outside, and he was just a dark presence to her, a shadowed stranger.

His lips weren't strange any more, but as familiar as if she had known their firm warmth forever, and when they found hers again her mouth fitted to them as if it had been made only for that purpose.

I didn't know kisses could be like this, she thought hazily, as he took her with him into the longest, sweetest, most arousing embrace she had ever known. His hands roamed her body, under her robe, not roughly or restlessly, but like someone discovering the shape of a precious object. Yet where he touched her, he left her flesh aching with wanting him.

'You're perfect,' he said huskily. 'Absolutely perfect.' He buried his face against her ripe breasts and then kissed each full pink tip.

'Oh, Seth!' It was exquisite pleasure, almost pain. Her body throbbed and ached with her need for him. Her hands ran over his wide shoulders, the slim waist and hard curves of his buttocks, then urgently shrugged away his shirt. She leant her cheek against his chest and felt the sprinkling of hair roughen her skin.

He held her while she helped him step from his clothes, groaning with pleasure as she knew the heart of his desire, yet holding back, patient, enjoying her touch.

It was this that made him so sensual, she reflected hazily. His ability to take time to relish each moment. Even now, as he pushed away her robe and they held each other naked, he was slowly luxurious as he pushed her back on to the bed, and it roused her unbearably. All she had known of lovemaking in the past had been a rough and hurried frenzy, often far from enjoyable, but now it was she who writhed against him as he kissed her eyes and ears and throat, then took each breast in his mouth, teasing and biting until she thought the lake of need in her would spill and flood.

She touched him, held the bones of his hips, needing him closer. He groaned and kissed her harder, more desperately, gathering her tight to him. Then he forced his lips from hers. 'Wait, Sophie.'

She flicked open her eyes, coming back from some far place, at the shock of his voice.

He stroked her hair, breath coming fast and ragged. 'I don't want to harm you, make you pregnant. Are you on the Pill or anything?'

She shook her head dumbly against the pillows, but he kissed her quickly and deeply, as if her reply had been a caress of pleasure. 'I thought not. Wait.'

She felt physically cold as he moved from her, as if she had been in her clothes and now she was naked, and the beating of her body began to subside. She turned and looked with wide eyes at his naked back. It was longer, leaner, more tanned than Graham's had been, she thought suddenly, and the thought made her blood run as cold as if someone had opened a door to let a chill draught of clarity stream over her.

She had told herself, never again. She had vowed she would not get involved with anyone, ever again. Yet here she was letting a total stranger climb into her bed. And what of Graham? Poor, poor Graham? How could she let herself forget like this?

Not that she ever could forget, not for a single day, which was why she had to live alone, and why this should not be happening, and it was all so unutterably, so terribly wrong. Her thoughts turned, muddled and wretched, and when Seth turned back to her her face was rigid with misery.

She wanted to shake her head, say, 'No. Not now, I can't. I've made a mistake,' but all words seemed to have dried in her throat. He took her in his arms again, kissing her ears and eyes and throat, stretching himself against her as his hand claimed the length of her slender curves.

But her body felt like wood. He kissed her mouth, searching to rouse her again, but she could not respond to him. There was a huge, raw ache of shame and misery inside her as she felt him slowly pull back from her.

'Why, Sophie? Why?'

She did not, could not respond. He rolled away from her with a frustrated curse and stared at the ceiling. After a moment he said flatly, 'I've drunk far too much to risk driving. You're stuck with me tonight, for better or worse.'

Now her shoulders were shaking and she had to struggle to muffle her sobs. Her eyes were tight shut when he turned to look at her, but when he put a hand

out to touch her face he found her cheeks wet with
flooding tears.

CHAPTER SIX

IT WAS morning. Sophie awoke in her own room, yet everything looked different. Her eyes went over the curtains, the bedside table, the carpet, and fell on her robe discarded carelessly on the floor.

Then she remembered. She turned her head sharply. The pillow beside her was dented but empty. Seth, and his clothes, had gone.

She turned on her stomach and pushed her head under the pillow as she always did when she wanted to evade uncomfortable thoughts, but there was no refuge there. As she stretched her body it felt strange to her, sensitised with unfulfilled desire, reminding her more clearly than any memory could exactly what had happened between the two of them last night.

How could she have done that? It was something she never did. Not with anyone, let alone someone like Seth Huntingdon. Yet she had, or almost had, which was in many ways worse, and she blushed with shame at her weakness.

The door opened. She shot up.

'Good morning.' Seth stood by the bed, naked except for one of her white bath towels about his hips. In his hand was a mug of coffee.

'I had a shower, I hope you don't mind.'

She shook her head, her cheeks still fiery.

He proffered the mug, watching her closely. 'I

wasn't sure if you were a tea or coffee person. I
guessed coffee.'

'That's fine.' Her voice was little more than a croak.

He came round the bed and sat beside her. One
hand moved to encircle her wrist but she moved it
away. She couldn't look at his eyes, so she was forced
to stare at his chest, muscled and broad and scattered
with fine dark curls of hair.

'We don't know much about each other, do we,
Sophie?'

She shook her head miserably. There was a lump as
big as a gull's egg in her throat, a ball of shame and
regret. He seemed to be waiting for her to speak, or at
least look him in the eye. When she did not he said
with brutal sarcasm, 'You *do* remember we almost
made love last night?'

His ploy worked. Her eyes sparked up at him, 'Of
course I remember. Why shouldn't I? I might have
been tipsy, but I wasn't drunk!'

'Why almost?' he asked her, his eyes holding hers.
He, too, was angry and his presence in her bedroom
was threatening. For a wild moment she feared he
might take by force what she had denied him so
belatedly last night, but all he said was, 'I'd like to
know what happened.'

'I can't explain.'

'You could try. Surely you owe me that, at least.'

'I don't owe you anything! I made a mistake!
Anyone can make a mistake!'

'Your timing was impeccable,' he said coldly. 'Just
on the brink of making love——'

'It wasn't making love, it was sex.' Her voice was
bitter.

'Call it what you will——'

'I made a mistake. It shouldn't have happened. I just realised it too late, that's all.'

His eyes scoured hers. 'Why was it a mistake? Why? We're two adults, with minds of our own. I didn't force you, did I?'

'No.' She shook her head, and put her hand to her brow. 'No, you didn't. It was all my fault.'

'Fault be damned!' he exploded and got up to pace about her room. 'Mistake! Fault! Why do you have to demean it all like this? It was honest. Good. We weren't hurting anyone. You're as Puritanical and guilt-ridden as a voyager on the *Mayflower*, Sophie Walker!'

'Maybe I am, but if I am, that's my business.'

'And mine, now. I'm involved whether you like it or not.' He swung back to her. 'I mean, how do you think it feels to know you've made a woman you like and admire and fancy like crazy as miserable as sin? How do you think it feels to touch her face and find she's sobbing her heart out because you're lying next to her in bed? I'll tell you how it feels! It feels like hell!'

'I'm sorry, I'm sorry! What do you want me to say?' She flung back the covers and reached for her robe, oblivious of how his gaze darkened as he took in her flushed morning beauty.

He sighed and ran a distracted hand through his hair. 'I don't know. All I want is an explanation. Sophie——' There was a tone in his voice, a rough command, which made her pause as she belted her robe and look up at him. '—just tell me, please, why did you cry?'

She looked at him for a long moment. Her lips felt dry and parched. She licked them, took a breath.

'I can't tell you.'

'Can't, or don't want to?'

She thought about the locked caverns of her mind, all those dark days and desperate sadnesses, the thoughts she could barely bring herself to face. What she was, and what she had done.

'Can't,' she said slowly, then because she saw his eyes flicker with hurt, she added, swallowing, 'not you, or anyone.'

Their looks held for a few more seconds then with an oath he turned away and flung back the curtains. Sunlight streamed in, dazzling them. He stood, fists on his waist, looking down. As he did so, a car came fast up the lane and skidded to a stop. He cursed again.

'Dearest Amanda has come for a Saturday morning visit.'

'She can't have! She never comes here!'

She shot over to look down. Amanda looked up. 'Get back,' she hissed at Seth, but it was too late. Amanda, getting out of her car, had already spied them both and was waving gaily. She sat back on the bed. 'Now it will be all over the county. Amanda's the biggest gossip from here to Worcester.'

'Half of it will be jealousy.' He slanted her a glance. 'You can take my word for it, there's a good few things Amanda has said and done that she wouldn't want her husband or anyone else knowing about.'

'If you're trying to tell me you've slept with her, too, I don't want to know!'

' "Too?" ' he taunted instantly. Then he snapped, 'I'm not telling you that at all. Only that the opportunity's been there for the taking. I wouldn't dream of taking it. In fact, in case you're interested —which I don't suppose for a moment you are—I'm extremely fussy about my private life.'

The doorbell rang.

'Shall I go? I could soon send her packing.'

'No. I'll have to brazen it out some time.'

She went downstairs. In the curtained living-room she saw the ashes of the fire and the remains of their picnic. She grimaced. The romance of last night was impossible to recapture.

'Amanda, this is a surprise. Come in.'

'No, Sophie. I won't stay. I can see you're—busy.' The innuendo was thick on her last word.

'Seth was just going.'

'No, Sophie—anyway, I only came by because I couldn't get you on the telephone——' automatically Sophie looked round and saw that at some point last night Seth must have taken the receiver off its hook '—and I wanted to ask you the biggest favour in the world. Although I wonder now if I should.'

'What's that?'

'One of my dinner guests has dropped out for this evening. It's completely upset my numbers. And since you're the only unattached female for about ten miles in any direction—the only presentable one—I came round to see if there was any chance at all you could step into the breach.'

Her thoughts turned rapidly. Normally she would have said no without hesitation—dinner at Bicknor Manor was something she enjoyed only as an occasional treat—but this morning everything was different.

'I'd like to,' she said quickly, 'but one good turn deserves another.' Amanda raised her eyebrows. She took the bull by the horns. 'Amanda, I've got my professional reputation to think of, and you know how small-minded people can be in the village. Please could you forget you saw Seth here this morning?'

'Of course,' Amanda gushed instantly. 'I under-stand completely, Sophie. You can trust me. Although, of course, if the two of you really are—I mean, word soon gets about in the country.'

'I know. But we're not. We're really not. Seth won't be staying again.'

'Oh, darling!' Amanda's instant sympathy grated on her raw nerves.

'It's my decision,' she rapped out. 'There's nothing to feel sorry for.'

'Well, I have to admit, that makes it easier for me.'

'What do you mean?'

'Tonight's dinner. You see, I had no idea there was anything at all between the two of you.'

'I don't follow you.'

Amanda had the grace to look genuinely embar-rassed. 'Sophie, I wouldn't have dreamt of asking you if I had realised before I came here. But Seth will be there as well, with his girlfriend from London.'

It was like a blow in her pelvis. Sophie could not speak.

Amanda scanned her pale face. 'It would save my life if you could come, but I'd obviously understand if you felt you couldn't.'

Sophie gritted her teeth. 'I'll come,' she said. 'I'll be there. I promise.'

And she was, prompt at eight o'clock, as stunning as

she could make herself in a favourite dress of midnight-blue silk, whose demure but flowing lines were ideally suited to her fragile, fine beauty. Even so, he was there before her, suave and handsome in his dinner jacket with a tall, sophisticated brunette at his side.

Her eyes went like lasers to the woman. She wore a red designer sheath dress and her hair was pulled back to the nape of her neck in a smooth chignon that emphasised the classic beauty of her profile. The diamonds at her ears and throat were real, and when she spoke to Seth she put a hand on his arm in a proprietorial way that sent an ache through Sophie's bones.

She wondered whether Seth kissed her ears and throat in the same agonisingly tender way she had experienced last night, and her eyes went to his and a look passed between the two of them that brimmed with all the anger and recriminations with which they had parted earlier that day.

'I think you two have met before,' said Amanda smoothly, and Seth took her hand and said something polite that she could not hear because of the touch of his fingers and the pounding in her ears. 'And this is Nina Nukana, the model. I'm sure you've heard of her. She's staying with Seth for the weekend.'

Nina smiled and held out her hand and Sophie forced herself to be polite. 'How nice to meet you. We don't get many famous faces in these parts.'

'It's lovely to be out of London, and I've been dying to see Sedbury Hall. Seth's told me so much about it.'

'It's beautiful, isn't it?' Sophie flashed a hostile look at Seth. 'It's a shame it can't stay the way it is.'

He smiled thinly at her. 'Without a roof and falling

down, you mean?'

'No, I mean as a family home—without jacuzzis and golf courses even as a joke,' she added bitterly.

'Jacuzzis?' Nina echoed, puzzled, and Amanda, whose social antennae had sensed the crackling ice in the air, hurried over to ease Sophie's path on into the crowded room.

Her partner for the evening was a young local farmer, whom she had already met once or twice and knew she had nothing to say to. As he described in tedious detail the state of each of his crops, her eyes could not help but stray to Seth. It was a strange and—she had to admit it—arousing feeling to know the shape of his body under the concealing formal dinner suit, but how deeply she regretted what she had allowed to happen between them!

Amanda's news this morning had come as the final straw. She had flung back upstairs and announced, 'I want you to leave now. This minute.' She had been glad to see that while she had been talking to Amanda he had dressed, although his chin showed the lack of a razor, she noted irrelevantly.

'Am I allowed the courtesy of knowing why?' His voice was as clipped as hers.

'Three reasons.' She ticked them off briskly on her fingers. 'First, what happened last night was a mistake. You caught me with my defences down. It won't happen again, I can promise you. Secondly, we've got nothing left to say to each other. Thirdly, I gather you'll be off to meet your girlfriend today. I wouldn't like you to be late!'

Her eyes glowed like an angry cat's as she glared at him. He was a liar and a cheat. A property developer who despoiled old houses, and a lover who cheated on his girlfriend. He had hypnotised her with his looks and his charm, but now the spell was well and truly broken, and she longed for him to be gone.

For a moment he looked as if he would argue, but then he seemed to give up the fight, at least for that moment.

'You look like a real schoolmarm, lecturing me like that,' he said cruelly. 'And if you carry on the way you seem intent on, you'll soon be the spinster schoolmarm it seems your ambition to be!' And with that he had left.

All day she had kept busy, ignoring what had happened that morning, and the devastating fact that two quite different people had made the same cruelly pointed remarks about the way her life seemed to be heading. Now at dinner she sat diagonally across the table from Nina, who she had to admit seemed charming, and soon found herself talking easily with her about her life as a model in London. What had happened to her life, she wondered, to turn her quiet existence so completely on its head? And her eyes strayed to Seth's dark good looks and she found her answer.

'And what about you, Sophie?' Nina asked. 'What do you do?'

'She's a schoolmarm. A spinster schoolmarm.' Seth's voice cut in.

Nina turned to him, obviously shocked. 'Seth!' To Sophie she said, 'You mustn't take any notice. I'm afraid he likes to provoke. It's one of his flaws.'

'I know,' said Sophie, and she glared at Seth so coldly that Nina looked curiously from one to the other.

'You two seem to have met before.'

'At this table,' she said quickly, just as Seth said, 'We've run into each other quite often around the place.' She shot him a daggered glance, sensitive to any veiled innuendo, but he merely smiled at her like a Cheshire cat. Her hands, clenched in lap, itched to slap him.

'Are you really a teacher?' Nina rescued the moment.

'Yes, I'm the deputy head at the village primary school.'

'Gosh, that sounds very important. You hardly look old enough, if you don't mind my saying so.'

Sophie smiled. 'I think everyone expects teachers to be as old as the hills because that's how they seemed when they were at school. It's like policemen—you know you're getting older when they start to look young. But I'm twenty-five.'

'Old enough to know your own mind,' said Seth pointedly, but by the time she had transferred her gaze to him he had turned and was talking smoothly to his neighbour on the other side.

Nina pulled a face at her. 'He's been as grumpy as a bear with a sore head ever since I've arrived. I just don't know what's got into him.'

'Maybe country life doesn't agree with him.'

'But you obviously prefer it to London.'

'Yes, I think so. I enjoyed living in London, but I don't think I could have taken the stress much longer. Although at the time I was simply bolting. I just wanted a complete change, and it seemed natural to come back to where I grew up.'

'That's how we know each other,' Amanda put in from the end of the table. 'We were at school together, although Sophie was terribly brainy and stayed on for years after I left. When I heard she'd gone to London I never expected to see her again.' She looked around her guests, smiling. 'She's a very dark horse, is Sophie. She never did say what drove her back here. I suspect a tragic love affair!'

Everyone laughed, taking the remark in the light-hearted spirit in which it had been said, but the words struck a raw chord and their casual laughter seemed to jangle in her ears like breaking glass. She looked around the circle of strangers, their faces flushed with wine, their mouths wetly open, all staring at her, mocking her. Panic flared in her breast, and took hold, like a spark starting a blaze. She looked at Seth. In the circle of jeering faces, his was the only unsmiling one, but he too was staring at her closely, his eyes assessing, his straight lips set firm against the brooding sensuality she knew could lurk there.

She got to her feet. 'I'm sorry—excuse me——'

From somewhere far off she heard Amanda say sharply, 'Sophie?'

'I'm all right,' she got out. 'Please don't worry. I just need a little air.'

And with that she fled from the room, out into the hallway, then through the front door to where it was cold and dark.

Almost immediately Seth was there, holding her shoulders. 'Sophie?'

'Go away!' she shouted. 'Leave me alone. Go back to Nina! That's where you belong.'

'What is it? You have to tell me.'

'Nothing. Nothing to do with you, at any rate.'

The panic in her breast was slowly receding. Her breath steadied. The dark doors on the past that had threatened to burst open spilling their painful contents were closing tight inside her head once more.

'Let go of me,' she said through clenched teeth, and he dropped his hands at once.

'Come back in to the warm.'

She shook her head forcibly.

'Why not?'

'Why not! How do you think it feels to have to sit there, talking to Nina, knowing that I—that we——' Anger made her look round at him. 'She's nice, I like her. I hate what's happened. You can obviously take double-dealing in your stride, but I loathe it!'

'Who said anything about double-dealing?'

'Good! Honest! Not hurting anyone!' Furiously she flung back the words he had used to her that morning. 'And then taunting me as you have tonight! Nina obviously suspects something. Don't you care about that?'

'What if she already knows? You should never jump to conclusions about other people's relationships.'

'There's not a woman in the world who likes the thought of her man sleeping with another woman.'

'Maybe not.' His voice twisted harshly. 'I obviously can't claim to know as much about women as you do.'

'Oh!'

'Sophie.' His hand caught her arm urgently.

'Sophie? Are you there? Are you all right? I've been looking all over upstairs for you.' Amanda's voice broke in on them as she hurried out of the doorway, then stepped back, surprised, when she saw the glimmer of Seth's white dinner shirt in the night. 'Seth, I'm sorry. I had no idea you were here. I didn't mean to interrupt.

'You're not.' Sophie walked determinedly between Seth and Amanda's flanking figures towards the house. 'Amanda, I feel very shaky. I'm afraid I'll have to slip away. I think I must have been overdoing it lately, or else I've got flu coming on.'

'Yes, of course. You must be tired.' Amanda's eyes slid sceptically to Seth. 'I'll get your coat. But are you well enough to drive? Shouldn't someone take you home?'

'Of course they should,' Seth said forcefully. 'Give me your car keys. I'll drive you over and walk back.'

'No!' Her voice was shrill. 'No, thank you. I'm fine now I've had some air. All I need is a good night's sleep.'

They went into the lighted hallway and Amanda called for Sophie's coat. 'Yes,' she drawled, casually, 'I can see that might be something you're short of.' She turned to Seth, raising her eyebrows pointedly. 'Something you might both be short of, in fact.'

Seth glowered at her for a moment, then turned on his heel and went back into the dining-room.

CHAPTER SEVEN

SETH telephoned repeatedly, but Sophie always put the receiver down when she heard his voice. He wrote to her, but she put the envelope in the bin unopened.

She threw herself into work, and after a time he gave up. For a week there was silence from him, and she told herself she was too busy to wonder whether he had put her from his mind.

The end of term was drawing near, and she knew that if she were to persuade Mrs Werner to retire it had to be soon, before the cold official letters started to arrive from County Hall. The head's increasingly erratic behaviour drove Sophie to professional distraction, but on a personal level she longed to spare the older woman the humiliation and shame that forcible retirement would mean to her.

After school one day she volunteered to help her clear the mounting paperwork.

The head peered at a letter vaguely, 'They want someone to go on a course—school management, or some such nonsense.' She let it flutter into the bin. 'I don't think so, do you, my dear? We're a school, not ICI.'

'I think you should think about it, Mrs Werner. There's a lot happening in education at the moment, and it's easy for a village school like ours to get out of touch. The education authority will strike us off their lists if we turn down every training opportunity. That maths course, last term, for example, or the computer one earlier. We should have sent someone. None of the staff is very strong in those areas. The inspectors——'

'Oh, those wretched inspectors!' Mrs Werner threw down her glasses with a sigh and rubbed her eyes. 'Did we have assembly this morning?' she asked, abruptly.

'Yes, of course,' Sophie said gently.

'I can't remember it at all.' She smiled. 'I do remember taking the top infants. We had a story, *Jack and the Beanstalk*. Johnny Edmonds wouldn't keep still.'

'He never does, not for anything. There are a lot of problems in the family. I've been thinking for some time that we should consider contacting the educational psychologist about him. I'm sure he's getting worse, and more aggressive with it.'

'Oh, I don't know. In the old days we just used to call in Father and read the riot act——'

Sophie sighed. 'These aren't the old days, and Johnny Edmonds has no father!' she said sharply. 'His father's living in Gloucester with another woman.'

Mrs Werner sat back, her eyes suddenly clear and beady. 'You think I'm out of touch, don't you, Sophie?'

Sophie took a gamble, desperately praying that a forceful line was the right approach.

'I think running a school is getting harder and harder. Lots of heads much younger than you are feeling the strain. You've carried the burden for nearly thirty years. Perhaps you deserve a rest.'

Mrs Werner sat thinking for a long, long time. 'Maybe you're right,' she said finally. 'Sometimes I can't even remember the children's names——'

Sophie's heart contracted painfully for the older woman, knowing how she had always loved her charges, and how she would feel that one thing more keenly than anything, but she pressed on, sure somehow the moment was right. 'And it's not going to get any easier. I know the inspectors are going to make some criticisms and we'll have to make changes. It's going to mean a lot of extra work for everyone,' her eyes flashed up keenly, 'a lot of administration.'

'Oh, how I hate paperwork! I came into teaching to teach, not to fill in forms in triplicate.'

'If you took early retirement, you could still help out in the classroom.'

'Yes, I suppose so. And I'm very tired. Life has been such a struggle since my dear husband passed on.' She looked reflectively at Sophie. 'There is nothing like a good marriage, my dear. A friend by your side for life. Life's very hard without it.'

'I'm sure that's true.'

'You should be married, having a family of your own. Or are you one of these modern career women?'

Sophie smiled, 'Mrs Werner, you've worked all your life! You're a career woman if anyone is!'

'True, true, I suppose. But it wasn't my whole life. The family always came first. Haven't you ever wanted to get married, Sophie?'

She swallowed. 'I was engaged once, but—nothing came of it.'

'Well, don't shut yourself away, just because of that.' Mrs Werner wagged a well-meant finger at her.

'Remember what we say to the children, when they make mistakes. You pick yourself up, dust yourself off, and start all over again!' She laughed merrily at her own joke.

Sophie looked down. 'If only it were something as simple as a mistake,' she muttered, but Mrs Werner's failing hearing caught nothing. She shook her head, as if to clear it of painful thoughts, and tossed back her hair. 'About this management course,' she said firmly.

Mrs Werner retrieved the letter from the bin and handed it to Sophie. 'Well, my dear, if you want to go, I'll make the arrangements. The old order changeth,' and when Sophie looked at her face she saw that the head's habitual lines of worry had been replaced by a new serenity.

She left school that evening feeling more cheerful than she had for weeks, sure that Mrs Werner would retire gracefully at the end of the school year.

She even whistled as she swung up the lane, and had the energy to look about her and note that the evenings were lengthening and the wild primroses were putting on a good show among the hawthorn roots.

But her mood changed abruptly when she saw a familiar black Range Rover outside her house, a familiar figure lounging against the bonnet.

'Please, miss, may I carry your books.'

Her good mood evaporated. Seth wore jeans and gumboots and a cabled cream sweater, all muddy, and looked as if he had come straight off the land.

She went past him to her door, rummaging for her key.

'You won't believe this, but I was passing the end of

your road and somehow the steering-wheel turned left
all by itself.'

'I've told you I don't want to see you!'

'I know, Sophie. I know. But I can't stay away from
you.' He rolled his eyes dramatically. 'I can't eat. I
can't sleep. I'm getting all behind with my work——'

She turned in the doorway, savage from the way he
set her heart racing, 'Well that, at least, is something I
and the rest of unspoilt Gloucestershire have to be
thankful for!' she shouted.

'Sophie, for goodness' sake, you're behaving like
one of your own pupils!' Angry exasperation drove
the humour from his face. 'Why won't you even talk
to me?'

'Because we've got nothing to say.'

'We've got plenty to say. You could tell me what
terrible crimes I'm supposed to have committed, for a
start.'

'You can't honestly stand there and tell me you
don't know!' His arrogance took her breath away.

'I don't know. I'm all ears.'

'I would have thought it was obvious!'

'Not to me.'

'Oh! You—you——' Fury rendered her speechless.

He came closer, walking up her front path, closing
in on her. There was no warmth in his face now, only
a dark gaze narrowed on her and a stubborn set to his
mouth. For the first time she noticed the lean planes
of his cheeks and the strength of his jaw, and she
trembled at his closeness, and his anger.

'You're a devious, two-timing liar,' she flung out.

'You've got no reason to say that!'

'I've got every reason.'

'Things aren't always what they seem.'

'That's what you say. But why should I believe you? I can't believe a word you say, and I can't trust you an inch. You're only here because you want to get me into bed, you've made that clear enough from the start. Well, you can forget it, here and now. It nearly happened once, but it won't ever happen again. Whatever brief thing there was between us is over, finished!' She scissored her hands wide to underline her words, wiping out their short fling as if it had never happened.

'If that's what you think about me, then it's clear you don't know me from Adam,' he retorted angrily, each word clipped and incisive, 'and if that's what you think about us, then it's clear you don't know yourself very well, either.'

'How dare you say that? What incredible arrogance!'

Now he was standing facing her, his hands pushed down hard into his jeans pockets as if to stop himself from striking her. She could see a tic of anger at his jaw and a gold glint of fury in his brown eyes.

'I know this,' he said, fast and low. 'I know that you're not the sort of woman who takes a man into her bed lightly, and I know that when we're together something happens that drives all sense out of the window. And I know something else, as well, and that is that when you froze dead on me the other night it was nothing to do with me at all. It was something you suddenly thought of, something you remembered.'

Hurt and icy fear at his words made her lash out like a cornered cat. 'Yes, you're right, I remembered the kind of man you really were! I remembered how you earned your living, and the way you treated me that first night we met! If I'd known about Nina then, I dare say I would have remembered her as well! You're just a taker, Seth Huntingdon! You see something you want, and you have to have it, and it doesn't matter two hoots who is standing in your way.'

For a moment she saw a flicker cross his eyes and he swayed imperceptibly backwards, as if she had lunged at him with fists instead of with words. His face seemed to be carved of granite, each handsome feature immobile and expressionless, and the only movement was his hair which blew waywardly about his forehead in the spring breeze.

'Have you finished?' His voice was like splintered glass. 'Because if you have, I could take my turn and tell you a few home truths about yourself. Like your smug belief that you're right all the time! Like your total inability to hear what other people have to say to you——'

'I don't want to hear any more. I didn't ask you to come here, I don't want anything to do with you. I'd be glad if I never set eyes on you, ever again. Please get off my path, out of my front garden, and leave me in peace!' And she banged her front door so hard in her face that she almost shattered its glass.

Yet for hours after his car had revved furiously away she paced the small rooms of her house, listening to the silence, and thinking she would go mad if she had to endure the lonely turmoil of her churning thoughts much longer.

The next day she made a decision and then a telephone call, and a week later, at the start of the

Easter holidays, she packed a bag and drove north to
stay with Florence, an old college friend, who taught
in a school on the outskirts of Manchester.

On the first night they sat in her tiny terraced house
eating a Chinese take-away meal and drinking red
wine while Sophie talked at length about the
inspectors' visit and the failing health of Mrs Werner.

Later Florence sat back and indicated the grimy
urban street beyond the window. 'Sophie, I'm thrilled
to bits you've come, believe me, but I'm puzzled as
well. This is hardly the place for a scenic holiday.'

'Scenery's lovely, but you can't talk to it. Anyway,'
she pulled an expressive face, 'I just felt I had to get
away from everything.'

'Ah hah! I smell a man in that sentence somewhere!'
Florence pounced eagerly. 'And not before time, if
you don't mind me saying so, Sophie.'

'Not so much a man. More a complete pest!' But
she caught her friend's eyes as she spoke and blushed
because she knew Florence would see the confusion
behind her words. 'And, actually, I think I do
mind—you saying it.'

'But it's more than three years now, since
Graham——' Florence stopped her protest when she
saw Sophie's face. 'Sorry. We won't talk about it. Do
you want to tell me about the pest?'

She described Seth briefly, and Florence laughed,
'But he sounds utterly wonderful! I don't see your
problem. If you can't find a use for him, send him up
here!'

'He's got a lot of charm. Enough to practically
charm me into bed one time when my resistance was
low,' she admitted candidly. 'But, Flo, he's a ghastly

speculator, and he obviously doesn't care a damn about anything but getting rich quick and having a good time! The night after our little fling I met him at a dinner party with his girlfriend who'd come down from London for the weekend, and he didn't seem the slightest bit abashed!

'He just tramples over everybody and everything to get his own way, and he seems to think that he only has to flash a boyish grin here and there and everything will be all right.'

Florence said, 'Cads are always the worst. The trouble is, they're also the most attractive. Who wants a good man, after all? They're always so dull.'

'I don't want any man. I keep myself, own my own house, have my own friends.'

'Mmm. I wonder if that's really true, Sophie Walker.' Florence eyed her sceptically.

'It certainly was,' she said bitterly. 'I was perfectly happy with my life until recently.'

'Yes, because you'd worked at it. I really admire how you picked yourself up after——' Florence hesitated, searching for tactful words '—after everything that happened in London. I know you wanted to be self-reliant, you probably needed to be for a time. But, Sophie, it's no way to live for the rest of your life. You can get out of the habit of building relationships.'

'I know, I know! And end up a dried-up old spinster schoolmarm!' She got up from the table and flung herself down on Florence's battered sofa. 'You know, that's exactly what he said. The most hackneyed line in the repertoire of any Don Juan! I'm surprised at you, Florence.'

'Well, maybe it's true. And, anyway, why not have a fling? Men do it all the time. If you like his company, if he's as stunning as you say, why not just enjoy it.'

For the briefest moment Sophie allowed herself the luxury of toying with that thought. Then she pushed it away. 'I couldn't do that.'

'No,' Florence conceded slowly. 'It's not in your nature. And the last thing you need is to be hurt all over again. But you can't go on living under siege from him, not when you're going to be bumping into him all the time about the place. Couldn't you at least make your peace with him? After all, when you analyse it, what has he done that is so very terrible?'

Sophie gazed sightlessly across the room, thinking.

'It's not a crime to fancy someone,' Florence persisted. 'It's not a crime to pursue them.'

'Double-crossed his girlfriend?'

'That's for him to worry about, not you.'

'He's as slippery as an eel. I know he's up to no good with this local manor house he's bought, but he won't admit it. He just slides round the issue by making jokes. When I tried to pin him down about it, at a public meeting, he made me look completely stupid.'

'How can you know he's up to no good?'

'I just know. I feel it in my bones.'

'Bones aren't always the most sensitive part of the body.'

'Mine are pretty reliable.'

But she frowned, thinking hard. His real crime, of course, was to have stormed her defences, to have had such a powerful effect on her that even here, a hundred miles away, the memory of his dark, seeing eyes made her blood beat with longing. That, and only that, was the reason why she had thrown away his letters and slammed the door so firmly in his face, but Florence was right. She could not go on like that. Far better, if she could manage it, would be to neutralise their relationship into a blandly meaningless acquaintanceship.

Florence came over and refilled her glass. 'Cheer up, Sophie. It's not the end of the world to have a tall, dark, handsome man knocking at your door. Think of me, and my short, tubby, fair one.'

She laughed, coming out of her reverie. 'Ben isn't tubby!'

'He is now. Look at this photograph he sent me last week.'

Sophie peered at the figure in bathing-trunks on a tropical beach. 'Good old Ben. He looks as if he's having the time of his life. Maybe we should have gone off to teach in the South Pacific, as well. Better than being spinster schoolmarms at home.'

Florence grinned, and plumped down on the sofa next to her.

'That brings me to my news. I'm going to do exactly that! I handed my notice in last week.'

Sophie's mouth gaped in surprise. 'Florence! And I've been prattling on about nothing. But I thought you loved your job?'

'I do. Did. Oh, Sophie, I've missed Ben far more than I ever thought I would this past year. I thought I wanted my independence, to do my own thing, but when it came down to it, I simply missed him all the time. It's so hard when you've been used to having your best friend around. Someone to make meals with, and go to films, and snuggle up to on winter's nights——Oh.' She stopped abruptly. 'I'm sorry. How tactless of me.'

'It's all right,' said Sophie quickly. 'So what are you going to do?'

'I'm flying out to join him in the summer. I think we'll probably get married out there. I'm sure the local headman could fit us in.'

'Oh, Flo, that's wonderful!' She sat up and hugged her friend hard. 'I'm so pleased for you. You and Ben always seemed so right for each other, I couldn't understand how you could bear to let him go off like that. I'm sure you're doing the right thing.'

'So am I, now. But I wasn't before. I had to have this year on my own to be certain.'

'Here's to you!' Sophie raised her glass. 'You and Ben!' Her smile faded. 'But I'll miss you at the end of the phone.'

'You can phone. It's actually easier than getting through to here.'

'Not on my salary.'

'Well, save up and come for a holiday.'

'I might just do that, you never know.'

Florence scoured her friend's face. 'I'll miss you, too, Sophie. And I'll worry about you. Promise me something?'

'What?' She felt a catch under her ribs.

'No, two things. First make your peace with Mr Speculator. You can't go on living under that sort of strain.'

'All right.'

'And, Sophie?' Florence's eyes searched hers hard. 'This is important, really important.' She caught her friend's hand. 'Promise me you won't get too bogged down in the past. I know how hard it must be for you, living with what happened, but life has to go on.'

'I'm not, Florence. I'm not.' But Sophie knew, even as she spoke, that she was not telling the truth.

CHAPTER EIGHT

SOPHIE found that it was far from easy to keep her promise, even that night, when she tossed and turned restlessly on Florence's uncomfortable spare bed, because faces from the past seemed to loom up and haunt her, and when she finally slipped into sleep her dreams were vivid with repressed memories.

It had been so good, at first, in London. She and Florence had become firm friends during the year they studied together, and when they both became involved in steady relationships, they had been delighted to find their boyfriends, Graham and Ben, got on just as well. When all four of them decided to stay on in London for their first teaching jobs, it seemed the most natural thing in the world to pool their meagre resources to rent one large flat.

It was hard to say exactly when the youthful joy of their student days began to evaporate, but she could remember so clearly how the first rifts had grown between Graham and herself.

She loved teaching, and took to her new responsibilities like a duck to water. She never minded staying late at school, or bringing work home. But from the beginning Graham seemed bowed down by the problems of the job, and took little pleasure in his new life. She was delighted to have a little spare money to go to movies, or out for inexpensive meals, but

Graham only wanted to stay in at nights. The warmth and humour that had originally attracted her to him seemed to fade almost daily.

He pressed her to marry him, saying they should look for jobs outside London and buy a house in a cheaper part of the country, yet the notion chilled her, and she pushed aside the conversation with a laugh, saying she felt far too young to settle down. Sometimes, in bad moments, she could still see how his face had looked at that moment—drawn and disappointed, with a dead light of depression in his eyes—and she wondered if that had been the start of it all. Because after that day, nothing had been quite the same again, and her life, which had been so carefree, tipped fast downhill into a nightmare so awful that nothing could have prepared her for it.

These days she battled never to think about it, and often she succeeded, but there were still black moments when Graham's gaunt white face seemed to hang before her, and his eyes beseeched her with wordless misery, and his lips began to open with a silent cry of despair.

'No, no!' She shot up in bed, shaking and soaked with sweat, and the nightmare slowly receded. That had all happened years ago, she told herself, as she reached a trembling hand to the bedside light. Florence was right, it was in the past, and life had to go on.

But Graham's life had not gone on, that was the terrible truth, and no matter how she tried to fight it, guilt and wretchedness still stalked like black dogs at her heels.

Even despite her bad night, though, she returned

home from Florence's refreshed by a week of friendship and support, and felt ten times stronger than she
had before her holiday.

So what if the very thought of Seth Huntingdon
made her quiver with anger and longing? She could
cope with that. She would be cool, but polite, and he
need never have the first inkling of how much he
continued to disturb her inner composure.

But the man seemed to have vanished from the face
of the earth. There were no letters from him on the
mat, and the telephone stayed silent. One day, about a
week after she got back, she bumped into Amanda
coming out of the health-food shop in the village high
street.

'Sophie, darling, you look marvellous! I was so
worried about you when you came to dinner the other
month, but you obviously just needed a rest. Teachers
get so tired at the end of term, don't they?'

There was an edge of sarcastic malice in her voice
which spoke of a continuing keen jealousy over Seth,
and Sophie was not surprised when Amanda asked
after him.

'I haven't seen him at all. I've been away, staying
with friends.'

'No one has. I heard he'd gone back to London with
Nina and there's been so sign of him since then. The
telephone is on the answering machine all the time.'

'Well, I expect he's got a million things to do, I
know I have. I'm sorry, Amanda, but I've got to rush.'

She kept a smile on her face until she had walked
away, but her thoughts were cast down. That was it,
then. He had gone away, with his girlfriend. And her
life was back into the same safe routine that had pre-

viously seemed so comforting, but now seemed oddly desolate.

In fact, the only good news was that Mrs Werner had finally taken the plunge and handed in her notice. As soon as Sophie had walked back into school at the beginning of term she had seen how bright and free from strain the head's countenance was, and her voice, when she announced her news, was almost girlish.

'Yes, I'll have a lot more time for my garden now, and to visit my little grandsons.'

'We'll all miss you,' said Sophie with genuine warmth. 'You will still come and spend time with the children, won't you?'

'Oh, it depends, my dear, it depends. The new regime may not want an old-timer like me around. And I've no idea who will get my job—although of course you'll be applying, won't you?'

'I really haven't thought about it. Surely I'm too young, I mean, I haven't had that many years' experience?'

Mrs Werner's eyes were suddenly clear and piercingly intelligent. 'Wisdom can go with youth as well as experience, and there always has been a maturity about you for your years, Sophie. I certainly hope you'll put in for it, and I'll gladly give you my backing, although I don't suppose that's worth much these days up at County Hall. I can't think of better hands to leave the school in. You're modern and forward-thinking, and the school needs that, but you value the best of the traditional ways, as well.'

'You're very kind.'

'Most of all you love and care for the children.

Anyway,' she continued, matter-of-factly, 'what harm can there be? Even if you don't get the job, it will be good experience for you to go through the interviews. Then you'll be better prepared next time round.'

'I don't know,' said Sophie, uncertainly, 'I'll have to think about it.'

'Or is there a man lurking in the background, about to whisk you away from us? There was a silly rumour going around that a friend had moved in with you——'

'No. No. There's no one,' she said firmly. Damn Amanda, she thought fiercely. Damn her! How stupid she had been to think she could ever trust her not to gossip!

'That's what I said.' Mrs Werner nodded. 'Gossip can be an ugly thing, but it spreads like wildfire. And although people's private lives ought to be their own business, well——' Her voice tailed off vaguely.

'You mean it could affect my job chances,' said Sophie bluntly. 'If word gets up to the bosses that I'm a scarlet woman, they wouldn't look twice at my application form? It's not fair, is it? A man could have affairs from here to Kingdom Come and probably be thought the better for it, but if a woman takes even the tiniest step off the straight and narrow then she's done for!'

'No, it's not fair,' Mrs Werner agreed mildly. 'Women have always been judged more harshly than men. But that's how it is, especially in rural backwaters like ours. And we are *in loco parentis* in our job, don't forget. We do have some duty to keep up moral standards.'

'My moral standards are perfectly in order,' said Sophie stiffly, 'no matter what they are saying in the village.'

'I'm sure they are, my dear. I have every faith in you.' Mrs Werner's voice was gentle. 'But I just wanted you to know how things stood.'

Two nights later the phone rang. Sophie forced herself to walk slowly through the hall, although her heart was racing.

'Hello? Sophie, it's Bill.'

'Bill.' Her voice was flat with disappointment, but he didn't seem to notice.

'Sophie, look, I thought I'd give you a buzz, because I'm seeing Jim Haines for dinner at the weekend. He's on the county planning committee, so I thought I'd prime him to keep an eye on this Sedbury Hall business.'

'Oh, that might be useful.'

'You still think that Huntingdon chap is up to no good?'

'Well, perhaps I've got the wrong end of the stick,' she said doubtfully.

'Perhaps and perhaps not. I thought it was damned odd the way he evaded the issue at that meeting.' Bill's voice boomed on. 'Only it would be useful to have a bit more evidence against him, if you know what I mean. And since you're the only one of us who knows him at all, I wondered if you could have another go at getting some information out of him.'

'I didn't get far that night, did I?' she said bitterly, remembering the way Seth had publicly mocked her.

'Mm, no. But that was all on-the-record stuff. I was thinking of a more informal approach, just some casual enquiries. I know you girls have your ways and means——'

'I don't know, Bill. I've only met him a few times.'
She flushed furiously as she remembered exactly what
one of those times had consisted of, and wondered
irrelevantly what Bill would think if he knew. 'I don't
have that sort of relationship with him, and I haven't
seen him for weeks. In fact, I heard he's gone away.'

'Well, see what you can do, will you, there's a good
girl? If we don't get any more details, we'll just have
to drop the whole thing for the moment, and that
would be a pity. It's these early stages that are often
the most important.'

'Yes, it is. And it would—be a pity,' she agreed, and
promising to do what she could she put down the
phone.

The acute disappointment of the call forced iron
into her soul. Anger at Seth surged violently up again,
as she saw in her mind's eye those dark, wicked eyes
and mocking smile. Why should he just take what he
wanted—from objects, from people—and get away
scot-free? He was the sort of man who would take a
girl to bed simply because he fancied her, and his
girlfriend was away in London. The sort of man to
turn a beautiful house into anything that suited his
purpose, without a moment's thought for the heritage
he was destroying. The sort of man who believed that
smooth words and a charming smile could mask a
multitude of sins. Well, they didn't, they wouldn't
—Sophie, personally, intended to do everything in her
power to ensure that that was so.

She had to wait till the end of the week, but on
Saturday she dressed quickly in jeans and boots,
pulled on a navy storm jacket to keep out the cold
needles of rain, and drove straight to Sedbury Hall.

The scrolled iron gates to the drive were closed, but not locked. She dragged one of them open and drove on up the gravelled drive. The front of the house seemed deserted. She stepped out of her car, pulled up her hood, and stood with her hands in her pockets surveying it.

It was a long time since she had been here and she had forgotten just how beautiful it was. Although small, it was graceful, its old honeyed sandstone mellowed with moss and lichens, and the mullioned windows set in perfect proportion to the façade. The studded oak door was shut, and her knock went unanswered, so she walked on, along the terrace that ran the length of one side, peering into rooms that were bare and empty, but showed evidence of much work to repair walls and floors.

Outside everything still spoke of decay. Weeds sprouted from cracked drainpipes, and the terrace was flanked by cracked and broken urns that had long ago settled at crazy angles. A few feet below was what had once been an intricate Elizabethan knot garden, but the box hedges had run wild and the beds had been choked by decades of weeds.

She stood and stared, oblivious of the rain that now drenched her, seeing in her mind's eye the house restored and the gardens reclaimed. She imagined children playing in the gardens, a family dog sleeping on the terrace. But it would not be like that, if Seth's plans came to fruition.

Anger spurred her on. There was a wall, with a door in it that yielded to her push. This was the back of the house. Outbuildings and stables, a kitchen garden, and a yard cluttered with cement mixers and builders' vans. Her heart beat faster. So major work had already started, despite what the planners had told the Conservation Society. Maybe they were all in crooked league together, hand in glove. What had Seth said? Everyone had their price. It looked as if he had found theirs.

She scanned the scene, blinking rain from her eyelashes beneath her hood. Then she saw Seth's black Range Rover, and her heart beat faster still.

Somewhere there was the sound of men working. She walked towards it, and soon found she was following a freshly dug trench. The ringing beat got louder, until she saw the bent back of a workman and the flail of a pickaxe.

The noise of the rain and the pickaxe must have masked her approach, because he worked without pause, even when she stood close. She watched him. Despite the rain he was stripped down to shorts, and his back and legs were wet with rain and sweat. He worked hard and rhythmically, the pick rising and falling and the trench extending steadily. For moments she was mesmerised by the sight of the gleaming muscles working together, like a well-oiled machine, the pick striking through earth and hooking away boulders.

Then the machine stopped. The man laid aside his pick and bent to haul at a loosened rock. Without looking up he spoke.

'Hello, Sophie. Come to continue our row?'

She gasped, in total shock. 'I had no idea it was you!'

'You disappoint me. I thought you were simply struck dumb by the awe-inspiring sight of my perfect physique. Ah, got you, you blighter!' His voice was cold, and he scarcely paused in his work. Even as he spoke he was panting to grapple a huge rock out of the trench. As he levered it over the side he looked up briefly at her with a keen, hostile glance that sent a knife of fear and longing through her ribs. He was begrimed, sweaty and soaking wet, but when she saw his face again, his lips set stubbornly, his hair plastered damply to his neck, she knew she had never been so fiercely attracted to him. It was like a scorching lick of fire, and she longed to put out a hand to touch the bare skin of his shoulder.

Yet she knew, too, that he was displeased to see her. She could see at a glance that, for him, the chase was over and she had been firmly put out of his thoughts.

'What do you want?' he asked bluntly.

'What are you doing?' The question was blurted out before she knew it.

'Drains. The very devil. And we can't get a trencher in here without demolishing that eighteenth-century wall over there.'

'But why you?'

'Why not? Saturday work costs double time, and I'm trying to keep my bills down. Anyway I enjoy it. It makes a change from shuffling papers, and it's one way of working frustration out of the system.' The pickaxe swung down hard into the soil. 'I've done a lot of digging lately,' he added with grim pointedness.

Then he stopped, bent down and pulled something from the slimy mud. 'Here, hang on to this.'

'What is it?' She crouched and took the mud-caked fragment, and as she did so their fingers touched and she felt as faint as if he had taken her lips in a searing kiss. But his face was hard. Hastily she stood up.

'I don't know until I wash it. We're digging up all sorts of stuff back here. I think it must have been the rubbish tip for about two hundred years.' He turned back to his work, leaving her standing foolishly in the rain. After a moment or two he said again, 'What do you want, anyway, Sophie? It can hardly be a social call.'

She dragged her eyes from the muscles of his back.

'I want to ask you, again, what your plans are for the Hall.'

'Who sent you? Bill Fletcher, I'll be bound,' he added shrewdly.

'Everyone in the Conservation Society is worried about what you're doing.'

He rested on his pick and wiped his brow with the back of his hand. 'Well, I'll tell you—again—I haven't yet decided.' A pulse beat at the corner of his jaw as he looked at her.

'I find that so hard to believe. I mean, you must have to tell your backers what you're doing.'

'I don't have backers. Only myself.' He spoke with clipped anger, then jumped lightly out of the trench. When he stood next to her she could smell the sharp scent of fresh sweat and see how his chest heaved as he spoke. Her mouth was dry. 'If you want to see my development plans, I'll show them to you,' he said grimly, and throwing aside the pickaxe he set off fast across the courtyard and down a track. He strode out so furiously that she had to half-run to keep up with him as he vaulted over gates and made his way across lush pastureland.

'There!' He stopped abruptly and pointed across a

road to a field where the turf had been ripped off and bulldozers stood around. 'Those are my development plans. Tell that to Bill Fletcher and the rest of his cronies.'

'But that's——'

'That's where I'm going to build the houses I talked about the other night. It seems you have to say everything ten times around here before anyone believes you!'

'No one doubts you're going to build them! It's the Hall——'

'You want to see the Hall? Right.'

Without another word he set off at the same furious pace. Half-way back she was forced to stop and catch her breath. 'Wait, I can't keep up.'

He turned, angry, 'And I can't afford to waste my valuable working time on pointless sightseeing tours!'

'I didn't ask you to waste your time,' she gasped out. 'You didn't have to drag me over there and back. You just did it to annoy——'

'So that you can match words to facts,' he cut in swiftly, and set off again, not looking to see if she was following, and not turning again until they were back at the Hall.

'Right,' he ordered rapidly, impersonally, 'you follow me, you tread where I tread. A lot of these rooms are still unsafe. And don't touch any wires or anything.' His gaze suddenly darkened and he smiled without warmth. 'Now it's my turn to say you can look, but you can't touch. The tables are turned.'

His furious pace continued as they whisked in and out of doorways, dodging scaffolding and negotiating planks. She saw beautiful panelled rooms and glimpsed glorious views from mullioned windows. The house reached out to her with an atmosphere of warmth and contentment, but there was no time to take it in because Seth was talking constantly, gesturing as he did so, and somehow her eyes kept straying to the flexed muscles of his arm and his expressive, lean fingers. Even mud-streaked and dressed only in soaked drill shorts and heavy duty boots, he was more handsome than any man she had ever known. His knowledge surprised her, too. It was clear from what he said that he understood every detail of the work being carried out, yet there was no time to absorb what he was saying because, having toured the downstairs rooms, he was now taking the gracious staircase two steps at a time to hurtle on through the house.

'Stop,' she begged, after they had whirled through two further rooms. 'Please stop.'

'Why?'

She gestured along the wide gallery, gasping for breath. 'It's all so lovely—but I can't take anything in.'

He stood with his fists on his waist.

'You wanted to see what was going on—I'm showing you.'

'You've proved your point. I can see you're not doing anything except restoration work.'

'As I said all along,' he rapped out.

'Well, are you surprised no one believed you? After all, you are supposed to be making money on this deal.'

'Am I? Who said so?'

'Everyone—it's common knowledge——' She

faltered as she met his granite stare, and tried to recall exactly what she had been told about him when they first met.

'Everyone except me. But I'm the last person in the world to be believed, it seems. Especially by you, Sophie!'

'Oh, can you blame me? Why should I believe a word you say? Why should I trust you an inch? Ever since we first met you've behaved quite outrageously to me——'

'And what about your behaviour to me? I've taken more insults from you in the last few weeks than I've ever taken from anyone before in my life. I thought for a time I deserved them. I thought it was a kind of long-drawn-out penance for that unfortunate first encounter, but when I sat down and thought it through I realised we were about quits when it came to treating each other badly. I might have teased you a bit that first evening, and I certainly should never have kissed you the way I did, but that doesn't mean I have to be cast into the role of arch villain and philistine *extraordinaire*!' His eyes blazed and his lips cut down sharply over his words.

'Why not, if it's what you are? All that talk about fax machines in the library and all-weather sports-domes on the lawn—it rang only too true to me.'

'Then why do you think I'm going to such trouble to repair the linen-fold panelling in the entrance hall and have the staircase balustrades recarved?'

She shook her head. 'I don't know. It doesn't add up.'

'Then I'll tell you why.' He stabbed an angry finger at her, emphasising his every point. 'It's because this house is one of the finest small Elizabethan manor houses left in the entire country, and I've been quite obsessed with it ever since I first rounded the corner of the drive and set eyes on it. And if I can afford to, I intend to put it back into the sort of shape it was originally intended to be in—with a few added twentieth-century comforts like central heating, of course.'

She searched his eyes. He wasn't spinning her a line, it was the naked truth.

'And then what?' she faltered.

He looked away, down the length of the gallery. She followed his eyes, taking in the lovely prospect.

'What do you think?' She shook her head. 'I mean, what do you think it should be used for?'

Without hesitation she said, 'It's a family house. That's what it was built for and that's what it should be. There should be children running up and down here, and a cat curled up on the window seat.'

There was a long silence, broken only by the tap of the rain on the windows at their side. She knew he was scrutinising her, but she felt suddenly ashamed, and unable to meet his eyes.

'Exactly,' he said coolly, after a time. 'Exactly that.'

Again there was silence, and the splatter of rain. She felt compelled to break it, compelled to go on.

'You mean——'

'I mean, if I could write my own future, that is what it would be. My family home. But we never have that kind of power over our lives, do we?'

She looked at him and saw a shadow of pain deep in his eyes and thought immediately of Nina, far away in London, engrossed in her modelling career. The urge to touch him was almost uncontrollable. To fight it, she anchored her hands firmly across her chest and under her arms.

He looked out across the wet gardens and said with cool matter-of-factness, 'However, I've got no desire to rattle around here like a single pea in a pod, so I'll probably sell it once it's finished, to someone with a hefty bank balance and six children in tow.'

'I'm sorry.'

He looked at her sideways, lifting an eyebrow. 'Spare me your pity. I'm enjoying every minute of doing it up. The future can take care of itself.'

'You certainly seem to know a lot about the technicalities,' she said quietly.

'I should, it's my job.' He laughed, mirthlessly. 'You see, the real irony of all this, Sophie, the final joke, is that I'm not a wicked property developer at all. You should have checked your facts. I'm an architect, and an entirely respectable, not to say eminent one at that. More than that, even. I'm an architect who specialises in the conservation of ancient buildings. You would scarcely credit the impeccable nature of my credentials. Why, governments around the world are queuing up to consult me about their castles and cathedrals.'

She stared at him dumbstruck, emotions battling within her. Part of her was so angry and humiliated that she wanted to beat her fists against his muddy chest, but at the same time he was taking in her wide-eyed expression and beginning to laugh, and somehow her anger was evaporating and she was laughing, too, giddy with relief at the new knowledge she had of him.

And as she looked at him her whirling thoughts seemed to make him spin out of focus, then back again, the same man but entirely different in her eyes, a man all of a piece, not the jumbled fragments she had known before.

'I've startled you,' he said, and his voice was no longer harsh and cold, but warm, like his eyes.

She shook her head. 'I'm dumbstruck. I feel such a fool. but you could have told me before,' she cried, accusingly.

'I didn't realise until today quite what a black picture you had of me. At least,' he added honestly, 'I thought your judgements were mostly based on what you clearly considered to be my base lechery.'

'I owe you an apology—about a hundred apologies—for the things I've said,' she whispered. Far more, she realised, if you also counted all the things she had thought.

He stepped dangerously closer. 'Just tell me one thing. If you saw me as such a monster, why did you let me into your bed that night?'

'Don't!' she pleaded. 'Leave it, please. I've already told me it was a mistake. I was very tired that night, and I'd been under terrible stress. The drink went to my head. Haven't you ever done anything you've regretted afterwards?'

He grinned, enchantingly. 'More times than I care to remember. But I shall never include that night with you among them. My only regret is the way it ended, the legacy we inherited. Sophie,' he took her hand and the feeling of his fingers made her quiver, 'I don't suppose you'll believe me, but I didn't actually set out to seduce you that night, not as such. I just had to see you, spend some time with you. You'd turned me into a man possessed. I couldn't get you out of my thoughts, my dreams. I still can't. I've thought about you so much I can scarcely believe you're here, in the flesh.'

As he spoke, he moved his hand lightly up her arm until he was holding her by the shoulder, his fingers gently stroking the soft skin of her neck beneath her hair. 'But you are, I can feel a soft pulse beating here.' He shifted, about to pull her into his arms, his eyes warm and inviting, urging her to tilt back her head so that he could claim his lips with hers.

She loved his face, she thought suddenly; she could look at it forever. She loved the straightness of his brows and the fine web of smile lines around his eyes, and the line of his lips. He was a handsome man, but it was far, far more than that. His face was alive and ever-changing, mobile with expression. He was a man who loved life, who laughed freely and allowed himself to get angry, and who was sure enough of his inner strength not to need to mask his thoughts or passions.

But she had that need, oh, how she had!

She reared back abruptly from his grasp.

'What does Nina think of the house?' she snapped out, desperate to set him away from her. Inside, her blood throbbed with longing for his lost touch.

He raked her eyes. 'She thinks it's fine.' He matched her tone.

Outside the rain was clearing and a watery sunshine was struggling to light the sweep of oak-studded parkland beyond the gardens.

'I have to go.'

'Why?' His eyes looked hard and bruised again. 'Why, Sophie? Why does it have to be like this? Forgive the arrogance, but I know you're attracted to me.'

'Attracted,' she echoed the weak word bitterly, not realising she was speaking.

'Why can't I touch you? Why, when I took you to bed that night, did you freeze on me like a spirit in hell?'

She stared at him, shocked at his choice of words. A spirit in hell. She had been that, and sometimes it felt as if she still was.

'Is it me, something I've said or done to you? Or is it something else, something in the past? It's that, isn't it?'

She was silent, incapable of speaking.

'It is,' he persisted. 'Something that happened to you.'

Her continuing silence told him it was true.

'Sophie, you can't lock things up inside you, they poison your mind.'

She put her hands to her ears, to block his words.

'You have to live for today. That's all there is.' His protests were hard, urgent. She could feel his eyes going over her averted head, and her heart was pounding as if she had just run a marathon. 'Why can't you talk to me, tell me——?'

Her head jerked up and her voice trembled wildly. 'If you care for me at all, one little bit, then don't ask me that! Never ask me that!'

He stared at her in silence for a moment, startled by the intensity of her words. 'I do care for you, more than you know. But it's wasted emotion.' His voice twisted savagely. 'We're stuck, aren't we? We've run up against a barrier you won't move and I can't cross.'

'You mean you want to go to bed with me, and I won't let you!' She held his eyes for a second, but then had to turn her head away.

'No, I don't mean that,' he shouted. 'Oh, hell and damnation!' A sudden smashing blow made her turn back. Seth had struck his hand down hard on the stone window ledge in frustration and was now nursing his hand, his face contorted by pain.

'Don't tell me,' he got out through gritted teeth, 'it was my own stupid fault. What an absolutely bloody morning this is turning out to be.'

'I'm sorry,' she said miserably. 'It's all my doing. I should never have come.' She could not bear his pain, she could feel it inside herself. 'Look, you must do something about that. Your knuckles are bleeding.' She reached out for his hand but he stepped back.

'What are you trying to do to me? Add torture to torment?'

Her outstretched hand dropped. She looked at him wretchedly. 'I only wanted to help. Can't we be friends?'

'Friends?' Again there was a twist to his voice. 'The last thing I want to be with you, Sophie, is friends.'

No, she thought wretchedly, you've got Nina for love and friendship. All you want from me is sex.

'Oh.' The wretchedness must have shown in her face because he put a hand on her arm.

'I mean, I'm far too attracted to you to pretend otherwise. It would be sheer hell for me to see those smoky eyes of yours, those flashing smiles, that silky hair, and to have to act as if I hadn't noticed.'

'I'm not in the market for anything else,' she said quickly. 'You have to understand that. It doesn't make any difference what flattering words you use.'

'Because of the past,' he accused her bitterly.

She thought of Nina. 'That, and the present.'

He set his lips. 'Well, that doesn't leave much, does it?'

She shook her head miserably. 'It would be simplest just not to see each other.'

'A simple form of torture, always the worst.' He held her look. 'Friends or nothing?' he said finally.

Slowly she nodded.

'Then let's try the friends,' he sighed. 'Whatever that means.'

They exchanged a long, bitter, wry look, then he took her elbow to guide her on. She pulled away, startled by the electricity of his touch. 'It means that, for a start, don't touch me!'

He dropped his hand with a sigh. 'I just wanted to show you the rest of the house.'

'You don't have to, you've proved your point. Anyway, I think you should see to your hand. It's already starting to swell.'

He grimaced as he examined the damage. 'Perhaps you're right. I've got some stuff in my room, but you'll have to help me. I'm no good at bandaging left-handed.' His eyes sparked wickedly at her, knowing it was just the sort of intimacy she wanted to avoid, but she refused to be drawn.

Side by side they walked back down the stairs and out on to the worn stone flags of wide terrace.

'This gets the full afternoon sun,' Seth observed as they walked. 'It's as hot as the Bahamas here on a sunny day. Look.' He led her over to the wall and indicated a sapling in the ground. 'They used to grow peaches here a hundred years ago. I'm trying to get another tree started.'

She bent to see small green leaves sprouting from new growth. 'It seems to be taking.'

His head bent low to examine its progress and as they straightened up together they were suddenly very close.

He looked at her in a way that made her lips grow dry. 'It's my gesture of faith in the future,' he said, with slow irony, 'since that's all we have left,' and even as he spoke he was reaching for her, drawing her into his naked arms and taking her lips in a deep, hard, yearning kiss that brooked no denial, and showed her more clearly than any words could the way he felt about her.

Resistance was impossible. His mouth mastered hers, as his arms tightened hard about her and drew her slender body up to the iron strength of his. His lips moved, searching her mouth, rousing her, sending her heart thundering like a torrent. A fierce ache of wanting spread out through her like a tree growing branches and twigs. The scent of his skin was a headier perfume than the most expensive aftershave, and the warm feeling of it under her spread fingers was as intoxicating as wine.

She felt his own fierce desire in the hardening of his body against hers, and her body beat heatedly in response, but even as she yielded further into his arms he set her away from him.

His eyes had darkened to black, and seemed to blaze down on her, and for a moment he could not find breath to speak.

'That's one kiss I'll never apologise for,' he said raggedly. 'Everyone is entitled to a proper goodbye.'

CHAPTER NINE

NOW they were in the kitchen, and Sophie was bandaging Seth's hand, which was quite the worst sort of start to their new, platonic relationship.

Every time her fingers brushed his a repressed shock of electricity seemed to pass between them, heightened by their mutual awareness that such sensations were now formally forbidden. It was the greatest relief when the job was finally finished.

He grinned at her, sharing her thoughts, as he surveyed his swathed knuckles. 'Thank you. The work of a professional.' He was sitting in a chair while she knelt before him. If she looked straight ahead her eyes met the scattering of dark hairs on his bare, muscled thighs.

She sat back on her heels and pushed her hair from her eyes. 'I took a first-aid course last year after we had a couple of nasty accidents in school.'

'You're very committed to your work, aren't you?'

'Of course. Otherwise I wouldn't do it. Life's too short to waste it on things you don't enjoy doing.'

'A sentiment I share exactly.'

She read the meaningful message of his eyes and looked quickly away, around. The huge kitchen was comfortably cluttered. In one corner was a desk heaped with papers and plans, while on the far side of the old flagged floor was a single bed.

'Is this the only habitable room in the place?'

'It is until they finish putting in the heating. In a month or so I'll be able to spread out a bit. Until then this is my kitchen, study, dining-room and bedroom. Actually I don't mind. I find it quite cosy. I do have a rudimentary bathroom.'

Her eyes went over the narrow bed. 'It must be cramped when you have visitors.' She hadn't known she was going to say that, and there was an ugly twist in the voice that came from her lips. She was not looking at Seth but he followed her eyes to the bed and a slight, triumphant grin fleeted over his face.

'Oh, you mean Nina,' he said casually, and his smile broadened. 'She was a bit taken aback at first. She's more used to the home comforts of Eaton Square. But she's a trouper at heart. She'll bunk down where she has to. Mind you, I get rather more creature comforts when I stay at her place.'

'Yes, I can imagine.' Images fleeted through her mind, but she banished them ruthlessly. 'Where do you live mainly?'

'Here. I need to be on site to supervise the work. In fact I've sold my London place—without the slightest regret, I might add.' He smiled as he quoted, ' "A two-storey penthouse in London's rapidly developing Docklands with stunning river views from all the main rooms." For which read a soulless two-bed flat with the smallest patio ever built by man, and stunning views of building sites and decaying warehouses.'

She pulled a face.

'Actually it was exciting when I first bought it, and the area was only just getting moving. There was quite a pioneer spirit among the first settlers, but after a time it began to get me down. I needed to see green grass and mature trees.' He grinned at her. 'I'm just a country boy at heart, you see.'

'When I lived in London,' she said, 'that whole area was just derelict. There was nothing happening there at all.'

'Where did you live, Sophie, when you were a city slicker?'

'Right on the other side, south of the river. In the dingiest flat you could ever imagine. We tried putting up posters and draping the lamps in pink scarves but nothing made any difference. The general sepia tones still predominated.'

'We?'

'Several of us shared the place,' she said shortly, and got up. 'Could I make some coffee?'

'Of course.' He nodded towards the Aga. 'Would you mind if I had a quick shower, or I just might die of pneumonia. Then we'll have a look at that thing I dug up this morning—you've still got it, haven't you?—and I'll show you the rest of the collection.'

While he was gone Sophie mooched about the room. On his desk was the beginning of a hasty note. 'Nina, here are the keys——' was the first line, but she could not read more because he came back into the room then, dressed more fully in jeans and a black pullover, and they scrubbed the 'thing' in the sink and found it was a silver filigree brooch, too bent to wear but still delicately beautiful.

'Here.' He pressed it into her hand and folded her fingers over it. 'It's yours. A present from your friend at Sedbury Hall.'

'Thank you,' she replied quietly, without prot-
estations, and her eyes caught his as she added quietly,
'I'll always treasure it.'

Now it had pride of place on her bedside table and she
often took it up and rubbed the worn, warm metal
with her fingers. Seth had offered to take it to London
to have it dated, but she did not want to let it go. It
had come to seem a talisman, a lucky charm for their
future friendship.

After that day he had telephoned her several times
and they had been together to see a play and an art
exhibition in Gloucester. There had been bad
moments. Trying not to touch each other, they
seemed to collide at every turn, but her enjoyment of
his company, of the chance to know him better, had
outweighed the frustrations of the evenings.

But their most recent outing had been further
afield, to Bristol, for a meal and then a late-night
showing of a new and much acclaimed French film,
and this had proved disastrous. The film had been
subtly but powerfully erotic, full of stifled emotion
and unexpressed passion, that so completely mirrored
their own suffocating situation that she had scarcely
breathed throughout its length, while Seth, beside
her, was a profile carved in stone.

Afterwards he had said nothing at all about the film,
but had driven her home fast and angrily, not moving
from behind the wheel as she got out at her front door.

'Seth?' she had said tentatively.

His face was hard and withdrawn.

'I probably won't see you for a time,' he bit out,
without turning to look at her. 'I'm off to the Middle

East on Monday, did I tell you?'

'No. You didn't.' Her voice was hurt and her heart plummeted. 'Will you be gone long?'

'I'm not sure. I'm advising on a major restoration programme, and it seems to have got bogged down with one thing or another. And when I get back I'll need to be in London for a time. I've let a number of things slip because of the Hall. I need to catch people before they go off for the summer.'

'Oh. Where will you stay?'

'With Nina, of course,' he said with casual cruelty, and his eyes flicked quickly to hers. 'I'll ring you when I get back.'

She got out of the car and leant down. Her heart felt like lead. She hesitated, licked her dry lips, then said, softly, 'Do you promise?' Her heart was thundering like a torrent. He turned slowly, a sensuous, withdrawn shadow in the darkness.

'If you want me to, I will,' he said, but there was neither warmth nor affection in the dark look he gave her, only a brooding look from his masked eyes.

Yet it was a month, an endless procession of more than thirty long days, before he returned, during which her quiet—and, she had to admit, increasingly dull—routine was punctuated only once.

Following Mrs Werner's advice, she had decided to make a pitch for the vacant headship. She was sure she would not get the job, and did not even particularly want it, but she knew it could do her career prospects no harm to be seen as keen to shoulder responsibility.

In due course she had been summoned for an interview before the school governors, most of whom she knew quite well, and who treated her kindly. But right at the end of the interview, when professional topics had been fully dealt with, one of the panel leant forward.

'Miss Walker, you live in the village?'

She turned her head. The woman, Mrs White, was a relative newcomer to the village, but had quickly inserted herself into various positions of authority. Sophie did not know her, but she knew she did not like the tight red line of her pursed lips.

'Yes, I do.' Sophie smiled.

'You live alone?'

'Yes, I do.' Her smile faded as her antennae told her where this line of questioning was leading.

'If you were appointed head of this school, you would be in a position of some eminence in the local community. You would be living in and among your pupils not just during school hours, but all the time.'

She nodded, waiting.

'Do you feel you could set them sufficient example?'

'I—er——' For the first time Sophie was flummoxed.

'I mean, do you feel your standards of behaviour are of the high order that would be expected of someone in this position?'

Spurting anger suddenly made Sophie's voice clear and ringing.

'My standards of behaviour would stand up against anyone's in this room.'

Mrs White's down-turned mouth expressed scepticism. 'You told us earlier in this interview that you were single and had no plans to marry. And yet I'm told you have men staying at your house.'

She flashed back instantly, 'Your information is inaccurate. But even if it weren't, it would be nobody's business but my own.'

'Are you denying that you have had a man staying with you as recently as last term?'

She hesitated. Thank you, Amanda, she thought, bitterly. 'I have many friends, of both sexes, some of whom stay at my house from time to time. I have done nothing while living in the village that could possibly be construed as a bad example to the pupils, and I confidently expect this situation to remain unchanged.'

She lifted her chin and from the side of her eye she saw one or two of the more friendly interviewers grin at her spirited reply, but Mrs White looked furious and she knew there was at least one vote that would go against her.

She scowled now as she remembered the exchange. Damn the woman and her pinched Victorian attitudes to life, she thought! And damn Amanda, too, for her spiteful, gossiping tongue! And most of all damn Seth Huntingdon and all the careless charm with which he had wormed his way into her house and her bed.

She was lying in that same bed now, tired from an exhausting day at school but with her mind racing too much to enjoy one of the novels she had brought upstairs with her, or to switch on the television.

Restlessly she stretched her limbs, pushing them out into cool corners of the sheets, thinking again about Seth, and his dark eyes and lips that curved so readily into laughter or set in brooding sensuality. Her body stirred at her thoughts, forcing her to remember how his lips felt on hers, and how he had taken her in his arms here, on these very pillows, covering her with the taut-muscled litheness of his body.

She blushed and kicked off the duvet, angry at the knowledge of the frustration he had raised in her. But even worse was the way he had walked in on her life, blowing apart the comfortable shell of routine she had so carefully built round herself, so that when he went away again she felt lonely and incomplete and longed for him to return.

At that very moment the telephone rang.

'Sophie?'

'Oh!' It was as if she had conjured him to life by the power of her thoughts.

'Are you all right, you sound strange.'

'Yes. I'm fine.' She swallowed.

'I just got back, about half an hour ago.'

'Did you have a good trip?'

'Yes, splendid. I held a few meetings, kicked a few backsides, saw a few new parts of the world. Sunset out in the desert, that's really something, especially when viewed from a Bedouin tent with a huge banquet laid out on the sand before you and dark-eyed maidens flitting shyly in and out of the shadows.' His voice sounded vibrant and alive.

'And what about London?' She voice was tight. 'How is Nina?'

'Fine, very busy. Off on a modelling trip to Madagascar. In fact, we only crossed tracks for a couple of nights the whole time I was there. She sends you her regards, by the way.'

Sophie was silent, seething, although whether with him or herself she could scarcely tell.

Here she was, mooning around like a lovesick teenager, while it was clear he had probably not given her a second thought between their last contact and this. He had made her weak, vulnerable, foolish, when what she needed more than anything was to be brave and strong, and she hated herself—and him—for it.

'I wondered if I could come over and see you.'

'Now?'

'It's only ten o'clock.' He was clearly astonished by her astonishment. 'I can't believe you're in bed or anything.'

'I am, as it happens. I'm absolutely shattered.'

His voice warmed. 'Even more reason for my coming over.'

'Stop it!'

'Sorry! I forgot! In fact I withdraw that remark completely and utterly. Consider it unsaid. Could I come and see you if I absolutely promise not to make a pass at you, not even to peck you on the cheek?'

She summoned all her will-power. 'No, Seth, you can't. I told you, I'm worn out, and I've got another hard day tomorrow.'

'Tomorrow night then?'

'I'm busy,' she lied. 'In fact, I'm tied up one way or another all week. I'll give you a ring next week.'

'For someone who made me promise to ring you when I got back, you sound remarkably unthrilled to hear from me,' he said shortly.

'My life doesn't come to a halt when you go away,' she snapped back. 'I do want to see you, but you can't expect me just to drop everything else in my diary.'

'You could do, if you wanted to enough.'

'I'm not that much of a fool, despite your initial impressions of me. Goodnight,' and she banged down the phone.

For some moments she breathed hard and held her hands flat down on the covers to stop them trembling. The sound of his voice had sent her heart racing, but she must not feel like that about him, she must not!

She lay back and shut her eyes, willing her mind to be blank, but the conversation churned relentlessly through her thoughts. For people who were supposed to be just friends they had just had a remarkable replica of a lovers' tiff, she thought, and her heart sank as she realised exactly how impossible it would be for the two of them to have the kind of friendship she had hoped for.

Finally she must have dozed because the sound of her doorbell jerked her suddenly awake. It went on and on, an angry buzz, that had her out of bed and running to answer it before she was properly awake.

'What the hell do you think you're doing?'

Seth marched in, throwing off his coat, hair dishevelled.

'I don't believe you're suddenly so busy that you can't make time to see me. I want to know why you're treating me like this.'

She turned without a word and ran upstairs to get her dressing-gown. He followed her unceremoniously up the stairs and into her bedroom.

'What's happened to you while I've been away, Sophie? When I left, you gave me the very clear impression that you were anxious to see me again. Now I find it's nothing but the cold shoulder.'

She flung round to face him, her robe forgotten in one hand. Her long frilled Victorian nightdress was decorous but she felt naked and exposed.

'What do you think you're doing following me up

here?'

'Looking for answers.'

His gaze ran over her face, searching her eyes, taking in the beauty of her fine-boned features. He looked at her tumble of hair, the hollows of her throat, the slightness of her figure in its voluminous white covering, and his eyes warmed and the tightness went from his mouth.

For the first time she allowed herself to look at him properly and felt suddenly weak at the shock of seeing his handsome face again. She had thought of him so often that the reality of his presence was almost overwhelming.

'Oh, Sophie, have you any idea how beautiful you look standing there like that?' His voice was both harsh and husky as anger fought with desire. He took a step towards her, his hand out, like a man approaching a shy deer. She did not back away, she could not, but stood mesmerised as he came to her and took her up in his arms. 'I know I shouldn't, but I can't not,' he said against her hair as his hands slid round her waist and tightened. She felt the strength of his chest against hers, and she closed her eyes as he buried his face in her neck and inhaled the sleepy perfume of her skin.

'Have you any idea how often I've thought about holding you like this in the past month?' he groaned, and answered his own question. 'Of course not, you've no idea, how can you have? Sophie——' He raised his head from her hair, and her eyes opened again at the sound of her name.

'Don't,' she got out, and put her hands to his shoulders, but his look was making her heart pound like a torrent, and even as she moved to push him away her traitorous hands were feeling the muscles of his shoulders and sliding down to hold him closer.

Then his lips were seeking hers, moving on them rest-lessly. 'Why?' he asked her, through his searching kiss, 'Why?' and she protested weakly against his rousing lips.

'You make me so weak, when I ought to be strong.'

'Good,' he breathed and he drew her closer, moulding her slender body to his, as his hungry, seeking lips settled into a kiss of deep passion, and his hands roamed her back knowing every swell and curve of it.

Breathless she turned her head and spoke against his shoulder. 'You mustn't,' but the scent of his body through the cotton of his shirt filled her senses and she could not move from him.

'Oh, but I must,' he answered, and his fingers thrust up under her hair to find the soft skin of her neck and to turn her lips back to hers.

Then she was truly lost in his embrace, opening to his kiss and feeling the strength of him holding her close until he led her to the bed, still kissing her, and eased her down and joined her instantly, his lips reaching for hers again.

'Oh, Sophie, Sophie, my love,' he groaned as he touched the softness of her hair and traced her face and ran his fingers down the parting of her nightdress to touch her warm breasts.

A piercing stab of desire went through her as he shaped them and circled them, feeling her flesh stiffen against his palms.

He raised himself back and looked at her wonderingly. She opened her eyes and saw how dark his gaze was and how dull colour flushed his cheekbones. His lips could have been sculpted in marble, she thought, they were so perfect, but there was nothing cold about this man. Emotions crossed his warm and mobile face like wind rippling a cornfield. Now he sought her eyes and his desire was written clear in every muscle of his face.

'No woman should be so perfect,' he said huskily and bent to kiss her ear and throat, his hand claiming her breast again. 'Such slenderness and fullness at the same time. It's too much for any man to bear.'

She closed her eyes against the desperate battling emotions he roused inside her. Her body ached for him, drumming its needs ever harder as his lips moved lower, sensuously exploring the curves of her body.

'Oh,' she groaned, and squeezed her eyes tight shut as if she would cry. 'Oh, please——'

Seth raised his head, looking at her, waiting. 'Please?' he prompted, in a low, questioning voice. She shook her head on the pillow, unable to look at him or speak. 'Sophie, look at me.'

Slowly she opened her eyes. He took her hand and drew it to his chest. 'Feel that. That's what you do to me.'

His heart was hammering like a steam train and his breath was ragged and uneven. 'I want to make love to you so much. I can hardly bear it.'

She held his eyes but no words came.

'You want it, too. Look, even the smallest touch.' He put out his hand and lightly traced the outline of her breast with his fingers. Immediately her body filled and stiffened with desire.

'No,' she got out, tightly.

'Yes,' he said. 'Your body speaks for you.'

'My body doesn't know any better!'

'Maybe it knows more than you do about what's best

for you. Oh!' In a fury of frustration he kissed her again, hard with desperate desire, his teeth and tongue punishing the soft inside of her mouth. His hands knew her breasts again, pushed up under the cotton of her nightdress to search her body and torment her to such arousal that she moved against him, closer to him, wishing only that he should fill her and complete her

But he tore his lips away, and raised himself back from her flushed figure, one hand each side of her spread hair, on her pillows. His breath rasped in his throat making his voice, when he spoke, harsh like a stranger's.

'It would be the easiest thing in the world to get you to change your mind, but I'd hate myself afterwards. Probably even more than you'd hate me.'

She said nothing, could not even open her eyes.

'Seth——' Her voice was small, tiny.

With a muffled curse he swung himself away from her, off the bed, and sat with his back turned, his head bent, his elbows on his knees.

'Damn it, Sophie, what are you so frightened of?' He turned, angry and disarrayed, and glowered.

She sat hesitantly up. His dark, compulsive gaze seemed determined to wring something from her lips. She knew he was at the end of the road she had thought, mistakenly, they could travel together.

'Involvement,' she whispered finally.

'What's wrong with that?'

'It's too hard to explain.'

'You've never tried.'

'No.' The past rose up before her like a black tidal wave. She shut her eyes tight against it, and it slowly receded.

But Seth took her angrily by the shoulders. 'Dear lord,

you make me want to do you terrible violence. I want to shake it out of you! Why won't you see? The feelings between us are good. It's a crime against nature to deny them.'

The voice that spoke, the half-hysterical scream with which she lashed back, she scarcely recognised as her own. 'What do you know about crimes against nature?'

His eyes narrowed, his voice was insistent. 'What do *you* know, Sophie? Tell me what you know!'

'No! I can't! Leave me alone!'

'I can't do that.'

'Why not?' There was an agony of hurting in her voice.

'Because we have a future together.'

'A future,' she echoed bitterly. 'You can't trust the future.'

'No, you can't. No one can. You just have to have faith.'

She knelt up, closing her nightdress with her hand. The worst moments of blind terror had passed. Now she felt only cold and empty.

'Well, I have no faith,' she told him bleakly. 'Not in anything, or anyone. I used to have, but I lost it. Now the only person I trust is myself, and the only future I dare to contemplate is on my own. I thought we could be friends, but I was wrong. Every time we meet, something like this——' her arm swept over the bed '—happens. We can't go on like this, we'll tear each other apart.'

'We don't have to! It's all in your mind!'

'That doesn't mean it's not real. Seth,' she implored him with her eyes, 'I don't want to hurt you. You must believe that. That's why you have to go.' He scoured her eyes. 'Go. Please. You have to.'

He gave her a long wintry gaze, backed by steel.

'I'll go,' he said finally, 'when you've told me exactly why it has to be like this for us.'

CHAPTER TEN

'TELL me about it,' Seth drove on cruelly.

'I can't, you don't know what you're asking!' Sophie's heart beat like a bird against a cage and there was a sick pit of fear in her head.

'I know you have to let it out, otherwise you'll go mad. You can't live like this, Sophie, like stone, like rock. Whatever you're holding there inside you is freezing you to death. Your body wants to live life like a normal, warm human being, but your mind rejects it. That sort of gulf can drive people insane.'

'I was all right till you came on the scene!'

'No you weren't. You were living like a hermit, like a—a porcelain doll.' He searched for words as his fingers pushed his hair back and his eyes raked hers angrily. 'You were going through the motions. Looking good. Doing your job well. Cultivating your garden. But you had backed yourself into a corner and then put up the barricades. You were only all right because no one was allowed near enough to see otherwise.'

'That's not true!' she cried, knowing it was. She knelt on the bed and his words seemed to pelt down on her like sleet and hail.

'No? Then why did you come scurrying back to Gloucestershire from London like a terrified rabbit? Why, since then, has there been not one single, soli-

tary boyfriend on the scene? Oh, yes, Sophie, I'm
sorry, but I checked you out with Amanda. Why do
sexual encounters seem to instil such desperate fear in
you? Why is the past a forbidden subject? And any
hint of commitment a terror beyond imagining?' He
stopped and his chest heaved with the force of his
words. 'Heaven forgive me, but I'm not leaving this
room until you tell me the answer to these questions.
Because I have to know—they've been going round
my head until I've started to think I'm the one going
crazy—and you have to tell me. You have to, because
until you do you'll have no rest, no peace of mind.
You can lock the past up, but it won't go away. It'll
just grow and fester inside you until——'

'Stop it! Stop it!' Her hands were at her ears.
'You've made your point. I know what you're saying.'

'Then tell me.' He stepped forward and sat with her
on the bed, reaching to take her hands in his. She
snatched them back, wild with the emotions that
raged inside her.

'Don't touch me. You mustn't. You can't. I——' her
voice cracked, 'I don't deserve it, your affection——'

'Why on earth not?'

There was a silence in the room broken only by her
heaving gasps and the rasp of Seth's breath. She sat on
her heels on the bed, her eyes bright with tears, her
hair in disarray.

'Sophie,' he insisted. 'Tell me.'

'No!'

'You have to.'

'I can't.'

'You have to.'

'I don't *have* to do anything!'

'Yes, you do.' He thrust his head into his hands and said quietly, 'Don't you see, we've gone much too far down this road to go back.'

She stared at his bent back in silence, her emotions in turmoil. The force of what he had said struck deeper into her heart than any other words he had spoken. It was true. There was something between them that bound them together, and every word they spoke to each other, whether in friendship or in conflict, every look, every touch, every breath, tightened the bonds still further. Even if she ejected him from her house tonight, he would still be there, in her heart and in her mind.

'Tell me about it,' he said, and his voice vibrated with low insistence. 'Tell me, Sophie.'

She felt the force of his will, bending her, breaking her.

'I can't,' she said again, and there were tears in her voice.

'Why not?'

'I—I don't know where to start.'

He looked at her and let the corners of his mouth lift a little, trying to warm her with a look.

'At the beginning?'

'The beginning?' She frowned; she could scarcely remember that, it had been so swamped by the terrible events of later.

'You were in London,' he prompted.

'Yes, when I left school I went to London University,' she said slowly. 'Then I stayed on for another year to do my postgraduate teaching certificate, the PGCE.' The words came out stiffly, like the voice of an automated doll.

He nodded, giving her time.

'I met another student there, Graham. He was a little older than me, a chemistry graduate. We started to go out and after a time it got serious. We got engaged at the end of the year.' Slowly the words came more easily. 'I'd already decided that I wanted to work in London for a year or two—it seemed to me that if you could teach there, in some of those tough city schools, then you could teach anywhere—so I found a job and moved into Graham's flat.'

'You lived together.' A dark shadow chased across Seth's face.

'Yes and no. It was a big flat so quite a few people shared it. You've probably no idea just how hard-up teachers can be, especially when they first start out, so it wasn't exactly like being married or whatever, but we did share a room. We were a thoroughly established couple.'

'Why didn't you just get married?'

'Graham wanted to. I——' She hesitated. 'I'm not really sure why. He asked me and I said no. I think I just felt too young. The thought of being tied down like that scared me.' She swallowed, then shook her head. 'It was after that evening that things never seemed to be right any more.'

She faltered. He took her hands. 'Go on.' His dark eyes, intent on her face, insisted.

'It had been a good year up till then. I loved my job and made some good friends.' Her eyes looked into the distance, the past. 'There always seemed to be a million things to do, plays and films to go to, parties at weekends. But then something happened——

'After I said I wanted to put off being married,

Graham gradually started not to want to go to things. He would say he was shattered, that he just wanted to stay in. At first it was occasionally, but more, until I got angry with him. We had a row one night when I called him a stick-in-the-mud, middle-aged before his time—all sorts of terrible things.

'He cried. Seth, it was awful. I'd never seen him cry before. He told me he felt awful, that he could hardly get through his day's teaching any more.

'I wanted him to see a doctor, but he wouldn't. He said it was probably some obscure virus and it would pass and things went on like that for some time. Then, one day, he tripped on the kerb and went sprawling on to the pavement, and a few days later he fell again, walking down some steps.

'He said his feet felt strange, as if they were half numb, and when I watched him walk I realised his steps seemed to drag a little.'

She looked at Seth with huge, haunted eyes, not seeing him but that kerbside scene again.

'I'll never forget walking back to the flat that evening. I knew something awful was wrong, I just knew it. It was like having a hand of ice squeeze your heart. He was exhausted when we got back, pale and trembling, and I helped him into bed. It was then I realised just how thin he'd grown.'

'You hadn't noticed before?'

She shook her head. 'We'd started to go our own ways rather. He was often asleep when I got back in the evenings, and then in the mornings it was just a frantic rush for school. Looking back, I should have seen so many things. But I just didn't.'

'So he went to a doctor?' Seth's voice nudged her

on.

'Yes, and he was sent straight off to hospital for tests. By then it was clear he was getting worse fast. His grip was weak and he seemed unable to talk clearly, but it was still about four weeks before we got the diagnosis.'

Her voice faltered again.

'Which was?'

'You won't have heard of it. It's called ALS for short. It's a disease where certain nerve cells start to die off.'

He shook his head. 'Is it rare?'

'It is in people as young as Graham. It's not that uncommon in older people, but you never hear much about it because——' her voice twisted '—it's progressive, and usually fatal, and most people don't live that long once they've got it.'

She heard his breath rasp in his throat.

'They didn't tell Graham that straight away. They made it clear that he was seriously ill, but they let him hope they could stabilise his condition. He also took part in some experimental treatment, and that gave him a lifeline for a time.

'I knew, though. I made an appointment to see our doctor and he told me exactly what was likely to happen. The worst thing at first was knowing he was dying and having to keep it from him.'

Seth's grip of her hands tightened. 'What a nightmare for you——'

'No, it was much worse for Graham,' she cut in at once. 'Imagine what it feels like to see yourself slowly wasting away before your own eyes! By Easter that year he couldn't work any more, and walking anywhere was a great effort. He needed more and more nursing.'

'In hospital?'

'No, at home. He was adamant he wanted to stay at home, in the flat. I think he knew that if he went to hospital he would never come out. I tried to look after him as best I could, but he was on his own in the flat during the day. It worried me. I tried to persuade him he ought to go to his father's house, in Sussex, but he didn't get on very well with his stepmother, and he said he wanted to live as normal a life as possible.

'Normal.' Her lips twisted. 'By the summer he was virtually bedridden, so thin and weak he could scarcely stand. It was terrible to see. He had trouble talking, and could only swallow a liquid diet.

'Our friends had been terrific, but most of them were teachers and had gone away for the long summer holidays. He grew very depressed.' She sighed, remembering. 'It was a dismal summer, always grey and raining. We had to have the light on in his room all day long. At one stage I read to him a lot, but the more ill he got the more he slept, and I'd look up after a page or two and see that his eyes had closed. I was glad he could sleep. When he was awake he was always bitter and enraged. By then he often said that if he had to die he wanted to die sooner, not later. He hated being a vegetable, but that's what he was really, by the end.'

'The end?' Seth echoed quietly.

'He died at home,' she said rapidly, 'late one afternoon. He went downhill very fast in the last week. For about three days he was in a coma most of the time. I sat by him, and sometimes his breathing was so shallow I had to lean forward to hear it. Then it finally stopped. It was twenty past five. I remember looking at the clock.'

'You were there on your own?'

'No, one of the community nurses was with me. They used to come every day to help, and for the last days they were there most of the time.'

There was a long, long silence in the bedroom. Finally Seth said, 'What a terrible thing for you to have to cope with. And at such a young age.'

She said nothing, still back in the room where there was no sound except the ticking clock.

'But it's over now,' he said after a long time, 'it's in the past. Your life has to go on.'

'How can you say that!' she suddenly flared. 'I haven't told you anything yet! I haven't even started! You see—I killed him! You see these hands?' She snatched her fingers from his grasp. 'They're the hands of a murderess!'

'Don't say that!' He was shocked, she could see it in his eyes.

'Why not? It's the truth. You wanted the truth, all of it. Well, that's it.'

'Why is it the truth? He had a fatal illness.'

'Yes, but when did he get it? He was a perfectly healthy young man until the day I said I wouldn't marry him. Immediately after that—the very day after —he started to complain of feeling tired.'

'Sophie, this is ridiculous.'

'No, it's not. I've got medical opinion on my side. I became very friendly with one of the community nurses who came to the house. She told me that although they don't yet know what triggers the illness, some people are sure there is a psychological basis.'

'Even so——'

'Graham was crazy about me, I always knew it. I never felt the same about him, even when things were still OK between us.'

'But——'

'I shouldn't have agreed to get engaged,' she said wildly, following her own thread. 'That was my first mistake. And I shouldn't have lived with him.'

'Sophie, you nursed him to the end. What more could you have done?'

'Oh, I nursed him,' she said bitterly. 'I cooked for him and changed his sheets. I put fresh flowers in the room and read him books. But I didn't do the one thing that mattered!' He waited, his eyes raking her face. 'I didn't love him! And that's what he needed more than anything.'

'Love wouldn't have helped him get better.'

'It would! I know it would! If he had felt he had something to live for, then he would have fought for life! But he gave in to it from the very first moment. I swear he wanted to die.'

'Sophie, this is crazy talk. You've brooded on this for so long that you've warped it all in your mind.'

'If only I had.' Her voice twisted with held-in tears. 'I used to smile at him, and try to be bright and cheerful, but he didn't look at my mouth, he used to look into my eyes, and they weren't smiling. Sometimes it was worse. I don't know what he saw. But I know I hated him being ill, I hated being tied to the flat, to his sickbed. I felt so angry with him sometimes——' Now she was sobbing wildly, racked by despair. 'You see,

Graham and I—— I wanted to get out of the
relationship, break off the engagement, I knew that
almost from the first moment we moved in together,
but I kept putting it off. Then when he was
diagnosed, I couldn't leave him——'

Great heaving sobs stopped her words. She drove
herself on. 'People don't change when they get ill,
they become more whatever they are. Graham wasn't
an easy patient. He was often irritable and demand-
ing. All the things that had begun to grate on me
before he was ill drove me to distraction afterwards. I
felt desperately sorry for him, but that summer, when
I was with him day and night, I thought I would go
crazy. Sometimes I hated him. And by the end I
wanted him to die, I almost longed for the day . . . You
see?' She raised her wretched face and looked at him.
'I wanted him to die, I willed him to die, and that's
exactly what he did!' And she flung herself face down
on the bed and sobbed, over and over, as she had
never allowed herself to do before.

She did not see Seth reach out his hands to her, then
draw back, thinking better of touching her at that
moment of utter misery.

'You did not kill him,' he said with quiet force,
staring with dark, compassionate eyes at her prone
form. 'You did not. He died of a fatal illness.'

'No! No!' She beat the covers with her fists. 'It
wasn't like that. I was there. I know!' Her words were
mangled by her sobs.

'Sophie!' He touched her hair lightly, but she flung
her head away from his head. After a long time she
managed to master the worst of her crying. Her sobs
grew slower, less tortured. Slowly she levered herself

up, and looked at him through eyes swollen with tears.

'You wanted me to tell you,' she said blankly, 'and I have.'

'When did all this happen?'

She shrugged, uncaring, 'Two, three years ago.'

'And you've never told anyone before?'

She was silent.

'Oh my poor, darling Sophie!' He shifted to draw her to him, but she pulled away like a wounded animal.

'I want you to go now.'

'And leave you like this?'

'Go, Seth, please!' There was a harsh cry of need in her voice that forced his respect. The need to be alone, to pull the covers over her head and drop into a deep, black abyss of sleep, was stronger than anything she had ever known. She did not want him to touch her, she did not want his warm, sympathetic eyes on hers. She did not deserve his sympathy.

'I'm fine,' she said dully. 'You don't have to worry about me. I'm not crying any more.'

He looked at her with shrewd scepticism, but slowly stood up from the bed.

'I'll ring you. Tomorrow. To make sure you're all right.'

'You don't have to.'

'I want to.'

'I don't want you to. I just want to be left alone.'

He gave her a long, dark look.

'I'm sorry, Sophie, but however much you want it, that's the one thing I can't do.'

CHAPTER ELEVEN

'MISS, miss, have you heard about the outing?'

The little boy pulled at Sophie's dress. She made herself smile down at him, although these days she found it harder and harder to find anything to smile about.

'The outing, miss. Jeremy Simmonds said we weren't going, miss. He said we weren't going in the coach, miss.'

The look on his face was pure anguish.

'I'm afraid that's right, Peter. The summer outing is only for the junior school. You see they're going to a great big swimming-pool with lots of whirlpools and big slides, and they only allow schoolchildren to go in if they are older than seven.'

Peter looked mutinous. 'It's not fair.'

'I know that you can swim well, but some of the littler ones can't,' she explained patiently. 'We wouldn't want them to be in any danger, would we?'

Emotions battled over his face.

'I'll tell you what,' she said impulsively. 'On the day that the juniors go on their outing, I'll try and find somewhere special for us to go as well. Then we'll have an outing, too!'

'In a coach?' he quizzed suspiciously.

'In a coach.'

'With sandwiches?'

'Sandwiches and crisps and apples and drinks.'

'All right then,' he said, mollified, and sped off down the corridor, brimming with his important news.

She turned into the empty classroom and sank down at her desk. She did not feel like organising a school outing. All she wanted to do was to go home to bed, pull the sheets over her head and turn her face to the wall. Sometimes she felt so tired she could scarcely put one foot in front of the other, and she knew why.

Immediately after her confession to Seth she had felt empty, her mind as blank as sand washed smooth by the tide. She had gone through the days like a robot, thinking and sensing nothing. Then feeling had begun to seep back, and with it compulsive memories of Seth's eyes and arms, the words he said to her. She longed to see him again, but all her energies were channelled into not thinking about him. Day and night she battled to keep him out of her thoughts, to not allow herself to know how she felt about him, and on the occasions he telephoned her she put down the receiver with a furious, 'Leave me alone!'

The last time they met she had cried out in anguish, 'You make me so weak!' but at that time she had scarcely begun to know the truth of that remark. Since then she had discovered it with a vengeance. Seth had broken open her life like an egg and shown it for the empty shell it really was.

Now her only joy was in her pupils, and even that was ebbing as her energy diminished.

'Lovesick,' she muttered to herself, under her breath. Before it had been only a word, a hollow conceit, but now she felt the power of its reality.

Love, though? Did she love Seth? She only knew that
she wanted him with a hunger that hollowed out her
body, she wanted to see him and hold him and touch
him. But she couldn't, and beyond that torment she
could not think.

'Miss?'

She raised her head. 'You, again, Peter! Shouldn't
you be playing outside?'

'I want to go on a picnic. On the outing. I want to
have a picnic on the grass and play hide and seek in
the woods. Somewhere with flowers.'

Her face softened as she looked into the pinched,
anxious face. Peter lived in a poor and overcrowded
house in the middle of the village and the only things
that grew in his back garden were the piles of scrap
metal that his stepfather collected and sold.

'Don't worry, we'll find somewhere. With flowers. I
promise.'

That night she rang Amanda who, she thought
bitterly, owed her more than one favour for her
gossiping tongue.

'Amanda? It's Sophie, I wanted to ask you a favour.'

'Mmm.' Amanda sounded uninterested.

'I'm looking for somewhere to take the children for
a summer picnic at the end of term. Just the littlest
ones. There'll be about thirty of us altogether,
counting mums and helpers. I wondered if you knew
anyone who might let us use their land. We need a
nice meadow, or park.'

She had hoped she might feel generous and suggest
they come to the Manor, where she knew there was an
extensive orchard and acres of wild woodland
gardens, but Amanda clearly still felt waspish about

her failure to deflect Seth's interest from Sophie.

'Well, the obvious person's Seth, isn't it?' she rapped out.

'Seth and I don't see each other any more,' Sophie snapped back.

'Oh? And I heard you two had kissed and made up and were practically inseparable.'

'We had a disagreement. A major one. I don't expect to see him again.'

'Oh, I see.' Amanda's voice warmed a little. 'Well, in that case I'll ask around for you. I'm afraid I can't help you because we'll be away in Barbados for a month, and you can understand we wouldn't want millions of children rampaging through the grounds without us there to keep an eye on them.'

'There aren't millions. And they don't rampage. They run and jump and skip. But obviously the last thing we would want to do is spoil your holiday, Amanda.' She slammed the telephone down angrily.

In the end, though, it was Mrs Werner who solved her problem. Walking into school one day she bumped straight into the headmistress escorting Seth to the school gate.

'Sophie!' she accosted her. 'I believe you two know each other. Well, kind Mr Huntingdon has just called in to offer us Sedbury Hall for the infants' outing. Isn't that marvellous? He even says you can use the grand hall if it rains.'

'Marvellous.' Her eyes flashed like knives to Seth who smiled blandly in reply.

'Amanda telephoned me to tell me of your little problem.'

'I'm sure she did.'

'She seemed to think you were too proud to ask me yourself.'

Mrs Werner had turned away to herd some straggling children into school, and they faced each other alone in the wasteland of the asphalt playground.

'I only phoned Amanda because I thought she just might be generous-spirited enough to let us use her grounds. You didn't come into it,' she bit out, 'one way or another! She just likes stirring up trouble!'

'Or effecting reconciliations? Let's be generous.'

'We have nothing to be reconciled about,' she got out tightly. 'We don't have a relationship, or a broken-off relationship, or anything else!'

He smiled a grim smile at her. 'If we don't have any of that, then there's absolutely no reason for you not to accept my kind offer to bring your infants over to the Hall for their outing, is there?'

She glowered at him suspiciously.

'You might find this hard to believe, but I actually like children. Nothing would give me more pleasure than to let them have the run of the place for the afternoon. Lord knows, the house seems empty enough with me rattling around there on my own, especially now a good half of it is habitable.' He stared down at her moodily. 'And it's not much fun admiring the gardens on my own, either.'

As she looked at him she could suddenly imagine clearly how it would feel to stroll through the thick summer dusk, with her hand in Seth's arm, and the scent of flowers in the air. She thought of tranquillity and love, of safety and home. Then she pushed it all away from her.

'What about Nina? Can't she help you out?'

'Nina is a lovely girl, but she's an urban animal. She'd have trouble telling a primrose from a petunia. Anyway,' he added briskly, 'this is all beside the point. Which is, if you remember, your school outing.'

'If you're telling me you had no ulterior motive in making this offer, I don't believe you!'

'Have I said that? Of course I've got an ulterior motive. I want to see you, in any way possible, and this seemed too good a chance to miss.'

'You mean you're going to be there?'

He suddenly challenged her with his eyes, hard and honest. 'I had intended to be, but if you tell me you don't want me to be, that you won't be able to handle it, then I'll make myself absent.'

She hesitated. He watched her teetering between fairness and self-preservation.

'I'm actually very good at organising children,' he added nonchalantly. 'I've always run all my nephew's birthday parties.'

'You have?' Astonishment overrode her other feelings.

'Why not? I told you, I like children. I enjoy their total spontaneity.' His eyes drove into her. 'Unlike adults, they always say what they think, and do what they want.'

'It isn't exactly like that—as you would find out if you spent any time with them. They are actually every bit as complicated as other people.' She glared at him with hostility. 'If they did what they wanted all the time they'd eat nothing but crisps and ice-cream and stay up till midnight watching the television. They don't get very far in life if they aren't taught self-discipline.'

'We all need that,' he said, 'but some people learn their lessons too well, don't they, Sophie?' And with that he left.

In the end, though, he was there on the great day. She had needed to telephone him several times over the necessary arrangements and during their brisk and formal exchanges, it had somehow become understood between them that he would be on hand to see to any unforeseen emergencies.

At school the excitement mounted to fever-pitch until the day of the outing finally dawned hot and clear, a perfect English July day, and the chattering children were herded on to their coach.

Sophie, wearing only a white vest-top and a floating Indian cotton skirt, nevertheless felt sweltering as she checked the final preparations, but when the coach set off down the green lanes of the countryside a cool breeze refreshed her. There were a million things in her mind, and although one of the major ones was Seth, she was determined to let nothing of her own problems spoil the children's day.

So when the coach turned up the sweeping gravel drive, and she saw him waiting for them, a summer figure in cream trousers and a shirt whose sleeves were rolled high on his tanned forearms, she determinedly squashed down the butterflies that agitated her stomach.

One of the mothers turned round in her seat and joked, 'Coo, Miss Walker, I didn't know you'd laid on attractions for the adults!' and another, looking long and hard at his handsome figure said, 'He ought to be on television. Just look at those bedroom eyes.'

Bedroom eyes. They had certainly been that the first time they had ever met, and that was exactly where they had led. Sophie looked at him quickly, felt colour rise in her face, and looked away, but when the coach stopped she was the first to jump down.

'Hello, Sophie. What a perfect day. The gods have been kind to you.'

'Hello. Yes, they have, haven't they?' They exchanged a look and she was relieved to read in it that he, like her, had decided to put their differences aside for the day.

Behind them an excited clamour rose from the coach. He said quickly, 'I thought it would be best if you settled under the trees down in the dip over there. There's plenty of room for games, but it's shady as well. I found some trestles and benches in one of the outhouses, so I've had them set up for the picnic on the terrace. Everything else is signposted, cloakrooms and kitchen and so on.'

'That you, you really are very kind.' She said it warmly and meant it. The Hall was a perfect setting for the children's day out.

He looked surprised at her warmth, and she realised with a sudden shock of recognition that she had power to affect him, just as he could hurt her, and that he had come to expect nothing from her but barbed words and waspish ways.

'I don't think you'll need shelter, but if you do the grand hall is open. I'd rather the children didn't go anywhere else in the house, though. There are dangerous floorboards and rusty nails they could hurt themselves on.'

'I think we'll be fine in the gardens, thank you. I'll

take them straight down, and some of the mums will set up tea—if you wouldn't mind pointing them in the right direction.'

He was right, she thought later, the gods had been very kind. From that first moment everything went perfectly. They played games, ran races and sang songs while over their heads the sun shone and the leaves of the oak trees rustled soothingly. The children hunted for last year's acorn cups, and the only tears were from one of the youngest girls, not yet five, who fell down and cut her knee during a game of hide and seek.

She sat her on the rugs spread under the trees and cleaned the damaged knee and stuck a plaster on it. Then, cuddling the young patient until her shock passed, she looked back up at the Hall.

It was a gorgeous house, so elegant and yet so unintimidating, a home, not a stately hall. Its rooms should be full of books and pictures, she thought, its kitchen perfumed with the small of fresh-baked bread, its gardens alive, like now, with shouting children.

Was that what Seth had been planning when he bought it, she wondered? Had he a mind to settle down and become a family man?

As if in answer to her question she saw him coming down the steps from the formal garden towards them. But he was not alone. At his side, laughing and happy, was Nina.

A pain gripped her heart and she tensed against the sight, so much that the little girl she had been nursing slipped quickly away, back to her friends.

Sophie got up and turned away from the sight that twisted her heart.

'Come on, everybody! We'll do "Farmer's In His Den" one last time, and then it will be time for tea.' Quickly the children grouped around her and she led the singing of the traditional rhyme, clearly and confidently, as they circled the chosen Farmer.

She had played the old games like these a million times or more with her different classes, but today on the grass, among the ancient trees, the little spinning figures seemed to make a charmed picture. They were more like spirits of children than children themselves, she thought, as they skipped and turned, and despite their bright modern clothes, they could have been part of any far-off age.

What she did not know, was how beautiful and innocent she herself looked as she stood straight and slender among them, with the sunlight and setting gold among her hair and her skirt catching in the breeze as she moved lightly in time to the tune. And because she did not turn to look at Seth she saw nothing of the unmasked look in his eyes, nor the way he could not tear his gaze from her, nor the way Nina rested her hand lightly on his arm as if to offer him comfort.

When the game had finally finished in a tumultuous heap of enthusiastic children 'patting the bone', Seth stepped forward.

'I've been delegated to tell you that tea is ready. Apparently the jelly is in danger of melting if you don't get there fast.'

'Thank you.' She felt warm and disarrayed compared to his crisp and cool appearance, while Nina in a short sheath of cream linen and a wide-brimmed sunhat could have come from a different planet. 'Maggie,' she said, quickly turning away to a young helper, 'could you lead them on up? They'll probably all need to go to the loo before they sit down. I'll clear things up here.'

Maggie's eyes were fixed on Seth, as if she had never seen a man quite so handsome. 'Yes,' she said abstractedly, 'which way do we go?'

'I'll show you,' said Seth, and engulfed by excited children he walked away, back towards the house.

Both she and Nina watched them go.

'Look,' said Nina, 'he's got a couple hanging off each arm already. He's a natural. Like you, Sophie.'

'It's my job.' She tore her eyes from Seth and began folding rugs and stacking games equipment. 'Although I sometimes think being a teacher is more like being a glorified char. You spend an awful lot of time tidying up.' She wanted to be civil to Nina, but her tone was clipped with held-in hurt.

'It's still a gift,' Nina insisted. 'I know because I haven't got it. Children terrify me. I never know what to say to them or anything.'

'A lot of people feel like that, but you'll change when you have children of your own.'

'Which will be never,' said Nina with such crisp certainty that Sophie looked up with surprise.

'Don't you want children?'

'No, no way.' Nina twirled her hat in her hands. 'You're shocked, aren't you? But it's true. I'd make a terrible mother. I'm far too selfish and self-absorbed.'

She bent back to her work. It was true Sophie was shocked. Shocked for Seth, for what Nina's blunt denial meant for his future, and her heart contracted for him, then hardened to anger at Nina's selfishness.

The silence went on a long time. Nina said, 'Would you like me to help you carry that?'

'No. It would ruin that beautiful dress.' Sophie quickly assembled an armful of things. 'I'll leave the rugs for the coach driver to bring up. I'm sure he won't mind.'

'Seth will do it.'

'We've put him out enough already today.' She set off, up towards the house.

'Sophie, wait. I've been wanting to talk to you.'

'I must go and help with tea.'

'It won't take a minute.'

Slowly Sophie turned and came back to face her. Nina opened her hands helplessly.

'I don't really know what to say, now, especially in a hurry. It's Seth—I'm worried about him.'

Guilty colour coursed through Sophie's cheeks. She prayed Nina would think it the effect of the afternoon sun.

'Worried?'

'He seems so miserable all the time, as if something's eating him up. And when he's not miserable he's just plain angry. If he had a cat he'd be kicking it from here to who knows where.'

'I'm sorry if he's unhappy. But I don't see why you're telling me.' Her blush deepened.

'I'd say he was a man in love—thwarted in love,' said Nina bluntly.

Sophie was silent, stunned.

'And the only candidate I can think of is you.'

Sophie's mind wheeled. Nina was talking quietly, yet she was accusing her of stealing her lover.

'We hardly know each other,' she prevaricated.

'It doesn't always take much time, especially with someone like Seth, who knows his own mind about everything, instantly, all the time.'

Sophie took a step towards Nina, forcing herself to meet the other woman's eyes. 'Look,' she said miserably, 'it's true we had one date. But that was just after we first met. I didn't know about you then, I swear. If I had done, then I would have had nothing to do with him.'

'Me?' Nina knitted her perfect brows, then burst into a round peal of laughter. 'Oh, Sophie, we're talking at complete cross purposes! It's my fault, I wasn't making myself clear. I'm not accusing you of pinching my man, just the opposite. Seth and I are the best of friends, but we're not a couple, not the way you're thinking.'

'You're not?'

'No, no. At least, to be absolutely honest, we were, briefly, about a decade ago, in our respective youths. But it never worked out, and it was all so long ago now I can hardly believe it ever happened. I love Seth dearly, but as a friend, nothing more.'

'But he led me to believe——'

'A ploy, I'm sure. He's desperate, can't you see?' She smiled at Sophie ruefully. 'He's not used to being rejected. I doubt if it has ever happened to him before. He doesn't know how to handle it.'

Sophies head was swimming from Nina's unexpected news, but she said suspiciously, 'Are you saying I should be nice to him just to salve his hurt pride?'

'Don't you care for him at all?'

She wanted to deny it, to keep the danger at bay, but the words would not come.

'I don't know,' she said slowly.

'Couldn't you at least try and find out?'

'I don't know,' said Sophie again, even more slowly. She was touched by Nina's clear caring for Seth, and the evident way she believed that she alone held the clue to his happiness. 'I'm sorry, but I have to go and help with the tea.'

Her mind was fuddled and racing, yet there was no time to sort out her thoughts, not now when the only important thing was to ensure that the outing finished calmly. She smoothed her hands down her sides as if trying to smooth down her thoughts.

'Lovely skirt,' Nina said with a smile that she knew meant the painful conversation was at an end. 'All those jewel colours. You've got a real flair for clothes, Sophie. You always look wonderful.'

Sophie smiled back. 'Thank you, but I always have to wear things that I can throw in the wash. I shudder to think what luminous pink felt-tip pen would look like on a beautiful dress like yours.'

They set off together across the grass and arrived at the tea table still discussing clothes. Seth glanced sharply at the two of them together but Nina smiled widely at him without pausing in her exposition of where to buy designer clothes at half-price, and although Sophie could see he was suspicious of their conversation, there was no shred of evidence that it had been about anything other than fashion.

She busied herself passing crisps and mopping up spilt drinks and was surprised to look up and find Seth, at the far end of the same table, efficiently engaged in exactly the same activity.

She paused, staring in surprise. She would not have

thought he was type to get stuck into the sticky side of children's parties, but he was working with a will, while the children—delighted with their new, important friend—clamoured for his attention.

As she watched, one nervous little girl accidentally spilled her juice into the lap of her new party dress, and tears filled her eyes. None of the mothers helping out noticed, but Seth was there in an instant, with reassurance and a batch of tissues.

Then, watching him, she realised it was all part of him, the same man who could be dark with passion and danger, or drenched with the sweat of hard physical labour, who laughed and worked and seized life with both hands, experiencing each part of it as fully as he knew how. And she knew, suddenly, that she loved him, and that she ached to be loved by him because if he loved someone it would be wholeheartedly, a total love, for now and always.

Then he looked up, over the heads of the children, at her, and the jolt of his eyes on hers was almost too much to bear.

Later, as the last stragglers climbed wearily aboard the coach, he caught her arm. His fingers on the bare skin of her sun-warmed elbow made her long to turn and throw herself into his arms. Instead she stood stock still.

'Come back, Sophie,' he said in a low, compelling voice. 'Come back tonight.' It was not a request, it was a command.

She fought to resist him. 'Surely everything's been cleared away.'

'That's not what I mean, and you know it.'

She swallowed. She was on shifting sand and the

tide was rushing in. Any moment she would lose her footing, slip and fall, and then she would be lost.

'I can't.'

'Of course you can. If you want to, you can.'

'You know why not.'

'I don't. I don't know anything. I want to know. Have to.'

Behind her the coach revved up. She became aware of interested eyes at the windows, watching their two close figures.

'I must go.'

'Come back,' he said again. 'I'll be waiting.'

She could not look at his eyes but stared at the cotton of his shirt. There were red marks on his sleeve where a small jammy hand had clutched at him, and the sight made tears spring to her eyes.

'Sophie?' he said.

She said nothing, but turned and climbed into the coach.

CHAPTER TWELVE

IT was still hot, even though the sun was finally setting. Sophie sat at her dressing-table and even the light towel anchored under her arms was too hot to bear. She threw it off and sat naked in front of the mirror.

Should she go? Would she go? She knew what she wanted most was the decision taken out of her hands, but she also knew that tonight Seth would not come knocking at her door.

He had made his position plain, and now it was up to her. If she went to him it had to be her own decision, taken coolly and clearly, in the quiet of her own room.

Until this moment she had felt almost too tired to think, but a bath had refreshed her and now she felt keyed up and restless.

She thought about Seth, and his dark eyes and warm mouth and handsome, expressive features. She had done him wrong. She had thought him a lecher, a ravager of historic houses, a two-timing cheat, but he had turned out to be none of those things.

How much easier it would have been if he had been. That way she would have had a good solid reason for having nothing to do with him.

She sighed and undid her hair and began to brush it out. It curled luxuriantly around her shoulders. Her eyes were clear and alive, her skin glowed from her day in the sun. She put down the brush and began to smooth moisturiser into her hands and arms. Her body was full and firm, the body of a young woman, unmarked by time.

Her eyes fell on a letter lying on the counterpane. It had been waiting on the mat when she returned this evening. As she had expected, she had not been chosen for the headship of the school. No doubt the thin-lipped Mrs White had had something to do with it, although there were doubtless other, more sensible reasons for her rejection, too.

The letter was friendly, even encouraging. She was sure that the next time she applied for promotion, or perhaps the time after that, she would be successful.

In fact she could easily see her life spreading out before her, quiet, professional, self-contained, just as she had wanted it to be. No pain, no hurt, no feeling.

She met her own eyes in the mirror. Was this what she really wanted? Really and truly? She thought about Seth, about his lips on hers and the way he made her feel. She closed her eyes and remembered the endearing fingermarks of jam on his shirt, and wondered what it would be like to have children of her own, his children——

Her eyes flew open. It was forbidden, a forbidden thought! Once she had never doubted that she would have her own family, but then everything had changed, and she had slammed the door hard on that cupboard full of thoughts and wantings. It was over, past. The chance had been in her hand but when she closed her fist on it there was nothing there but air. Life was treacherous. It robbed you of the things you held most dear and pushed you to do terrible things you never thought you were capable of. The only way to make sure it didn't was to rely on nothing and no one but yourself.

Abruptly she banged down the bottle of cream and stood up, pacing restlessly. How could she even think of going to Seth tonight? She pulled on a robe and threw open the windows longing for air. But the thundery summer twilight was as hot and heavy as a blanket. She flung herself down on the bed and stared at the ceiling.

He was waiting for her. She could almost feel it like a pulse in the air. Somewhere he was sitting, or lying, or pacing, and his thoughts were on her, willing her to come to him.

She sat up again and the very walls of the room seemed to close in about her, pushing her out. She could not breathe. If she stayed here, she suddenly knew, she would be suffocated alive by their safety and emptiness.

With one swift movement she swung down from the bed and began to dress, just a purple slip of a dress, Indian cotton again and as light as a feather. She put on her make-up, not allowing herself to think, slipped on her shoes and picked up her bag.

As she drove her blood pounded in her ears. If she dared to let herself think she would have to stop, turn round, go home. So she put a cassette of driving rock music into the car's tape-deck and put her foot down hard to the floor. Fast and furious she drove along the country lanes, the hedgerows slipping past her eyes at frightening speed until at last the gated entrance to Sedbury Hall, open, loomed up.

She turned into the drive and pulled up outside the house, blood drumming, her heart hammering. Light spilled on to the gravel from the mullioned windows, but the oak door stayed shut. She let the engine and the music die away into the silent country night, surprised he had not come to greet her. In her mind she had pictured a headlong, passionate embrace, with no time for words or thoughts. Now it seemed she had to knock meekly and wait to be admitted, like any normal visitor.

'You came.' His voice was quiet. She whirled around. Part of the dusky shadows had detached itself and walked slowly towards her. 'I couldn't bear to stay indoors tonight. I've been walking the gardens.'

'You made me.' She hadn't known she was going to say that. 'I didn't mean to, but I could almost feel you willing me to come.'

He smiled, she saw a brief gleam of teeth in the darkness.

'I hoped you would come,' he corrected. 'I don't have any supernatural powers.'

But he did, she thought, he had the power to lay trails of desire along her skin just by speaking to her in that dark voice.

She said nothing.

'Come.' He held out his hand. 'Come and walk with me,' and he grasped her hand in his and led her away from the house down through the formal terraces to a part of the gardens she had not seen before where old-fashioned roses, long run riot, scented the air with their falling richness.

For a long time they scarcely spoke, until the mad beating of her heart had calmed and she could no longer remember what she had been so frightened of, or why she had ever doubted she should come.

The cool firmness of his hand and the measured pace of their strolling seemed to recharge her strength, and after the bustle of her long day's work the dusky silence of the hot and heavy night was bliss.

After a time they began to speak quietly of this and that, the bats that skimmed across their path, or the luminous white glow of a particular flower, but everything that mattered was left unsaid. Thunder rolled somewhere a long way off.

This isn't it, she thought to herself, this isn't real. This calm is only temporary and the peace an illusion. But it was blissful, and she sank herself deep into the joy of the moment.

After a long time, they circled back until the house came into view again. The blaze of light from its windows showed how thick the darkness had grown, but the heat had scarcely lessened and the growls of thunder were louder.

'We'll have a storm later,' said Seth, as they mounted the stairs to the terrace, 'but it should hold off for a while. Have you eaten?'

She shook her head, and he smiled at her quietness.

'I left one of this afternoon's tables out, I thought we could eat out here. Don't worry, I cleaned all the oranges juice and crisps off it.'

'I'm not very hungry.'

'Avocado,' he tempted her, 'with crab. A salad, and some of Gloucester's best bread. Light and nourishing. You ought to eat, you've been working like a slave all day.'

With the help of a white damask cloth and a silver

candelabrum he had turned the functional trestle into a luxurious dining-table. Cane chairs had replaced the children's benches, wine cooled in a bucket, and the food was spread out temptingly. Away from the shelter of the darkness she felt panic begin to return. She could see more of Seth, see how he had changed into a fresh white shirt and dark trousers, see how his eyes lingered sensually on her bare shoulders.

'You presumed I'd come!' she accused him.

'No, I hoped.'

He poured them both wine and raised his glass to her but she was glad he proposed no easy, facile toast. What lay ahead for them was all still unknown.

'Where is Nina?'

'She went back to London this afternoon.' He eyed her over his glass. 'You two seemed to have a lot to say to each other this afternoon.'

'She told me where to shop in London.'

'And that's all?' He raised an eyebrow. The thunder rumbled again. The peace was ending, she thought, the calm would soon be broken now.

'No.' She looked up at him. 'She told me she wasn't your girlfriend, that she hadn't been for years.'

'I never said she was.'

'You hardly made it clear she wasn't!'

'There seemed to be no reason to.'

'That first night we——' She corrected herself hastily. 'That night you stayed at my house. Afterwards I thought you had been playing around while her back was turned, two-timing us both.'

'I could have easily put you right, if you'd let me speak to you, but you didn't. And after that we were "just good friends", if you remember.' His voice hardened.

She swallowed, looked at him openly. 'That was a mistake. I admit it. We could never be friends. Not in a million years.'

'Then what are we now?' he asked in a low voice.

She stared at her plate miserably. Why did he make it so hard? Why was he trying to force words from her mouth? If only he would just take her in his arms she would be lost.

After a long time he sighed, then pressed her to eat, and after the first difficult mouthfuls she found it surprisingly easy to manage a small meal.

'The children had a good time, anyway,' he said abruptly, in an apparent *non sequitur*.

'They had a wonderful time. It was so good of you to let them come. They want to write you thank-you notes in class next week. It was their own idea.'

'I shall look forward to that. Will you be the post-mistress?' He challenged her with a warm and hungry look, his first open flirtation of the evening.

'Don't!' she burst out, panic hammering in her pulses. 'Don't,' she repeated more quietly.

Now his patience began to crack. 'Don't what? Don't look at you! For heaven's sake, Sophie, you're as jumpy as an overbred racing colt. I feel as if one false word will send you cantering off to your car.'

'I'm sorry.' Lightning suddenly flickered luridly along the horizon, making them both turn and jump.

He ran a distracted hand through his hair, then sighed. 'Strawberries, quickly,' he said, pushing a glass dish across to her, 'before the heavens open. There's time enough to make ourselves wretched later.'

She stared at him.

'Wretched?'

'Yes, wretched. As miserable as bloody sin. How else do you want me to put it? At least, I am. I don't have the first clue what you feel.'

'You? Because of me?'

'Yes, me, because of you.' His voice was curt. 'It can't be any great surprise. I haven't exactly made any secret of my feelings.'

'I knew you wanted to——' She shrugged with embarrassment. 'I didn't—oh, I don't know!'

'Well, you do now!' He ran his hand through his hair again. 'This is impossible. Why did you come tonight, Sophie?'

She struggled for words, in vain.

'I want you to tell me,' he drove on cruelly. 'It's got to come from you, don't you see?' He reached for her hand across the table, and his touch was like fire. Suppose I got up now, came round to you, lifted you up into my arms. What would happen?' Her eyes were on his, wide. He answered his own question. 'But we already know the answer to that, don't we? We've been there before. We set each other aflame like the Great Fire of London! Sophie, I don't know about you, but it's never been like this for me before. I used to read about people being mad with desire, losing their heads, all those clichés, but I never believed it. I was always in control before, always able to turn it on, or turn it off, as the moment dictated. But from the first moment with you it was different. It was all I could do to keep myself from ravishing you in a ditch on the way home from dinner. I tell you, I frightened myself.'

'It's nothing to what you did to me.'

He smiled a little, then grew immediately serious again, and his voice roughened. 'But then what? At some point, sooner or later, you would, as I'm sure you'd put it to yourself, "come to your senses". Your mind would take over and tell you to act sensibly, and you'd push me away and slam those hatches down again.' He paused and sighed, looking at her intently. 'And those maddening eyes of yours would turn from smoky blue to hostile grey and you'd look at me as if I were some species of sub-life that you'd dredged up from the bottom of the pond, and make me feel that whatever had just taken place between us was nothing more than the product of my base lusts——'

'Stop it! You make me sound like some terrible Gorgon.'

He shrugged. There was silence, except for the thunder growling nearer.

'It's true that we're attracted to each other,' she said weakly, after a time.

He swept her words aside with a blunt curse.

'Well, what do you want me to say?' she burst out, drawing her hand back sharply from his grip. 'Everything you've just said is true! We should just stay out of each other's way completely.'

'Why?' He was shaking his hand, shouting in frustrated fury. 'I don't understand. Just tell me why.'

'You know why!'

'No, I don't.'

'But I told you——'

'You told me nothing that amounts to any good reason for us not to be involved!'

'How can you say that!'

'Easily. Shall I say it again?'

'No! Don't you see——'

'I don't see anything, unless there's something you still haven't told me. Are you married?' He was angry. The words rapped out furiously.

'No!'

'Engaged?'

'No! How can you even ask me that?'

'A nun?' he cut in.

'No!'

The air around her seemed to grow thicker with every question. She fought for breath in the sultry night, and tendrils of curls clung to her damp skin as she tossed her head from side to side. Now the lightning was dancing in sheets and thunder rolled so loudly that it almost obscured their words.

'Don't, Seth, don't do this to me! Please!' she begged him, her hands at her head. 'I shouldn't have come tonight!'

'But you did,' he said relentlessly. 'Why?'

'I don't know.' She felt sobs rising in her throat. 'I don't know. I don't know.'

'You came because you had to. We don't have to play games any more, Sophie. You want me every bit as much as I want you. It's torment for us to be together and not touch each other. I saw how you looked at me this afternoon, when you saw Nina by my side. I don't know if you saw how I looked at you when you were singing with the children. You had the sun in your hair, and you were so lithe and slender . . . Damn it!' He drove his fist down hard on the table. 'I don't think I've ever seen a woman look more beautiful!'

She looked at him helplessly. Beneath the table her hands were crumpling the edge of the cloth into a ball of creases.

'I've never felt about anyone before as I feel about you,' he said. 'Yet every time I try to get near you you back away from me. I know you've been hurt, I know how you've suffered. But why won't you let me hold you, comfort you? What do I have to do to break through those barriers?'

'You don't have to do anything.'

As she spoke lightning lit his face, showing angry, naked emotion.

He waited but when she said nothing he burst out savagely, 'You know your trouble, Sophie? You're living in a nightmare of your own making! You're frozen in the past, and it's slowly chilling you to death. You've got to let it go or your life won't be worth living.'

'Don't say that! I've got my work, my home, my friends. Just because I'm not looking for a raging affair——'

He dismissed this with an angry snort. 'It's not that you're not looking. It's that you run a million miles from the first hint of one! You're a passionate woman, Sophie, yet you deny it to yourself and everyone else. All that repression, all that holding back. It's just storing up trouble for yourself in the future. Where's it going to lead? Have you thought of that?'

'Oh!' It came out as a furious, tearful gasp.

He drove on, in a torrent of words, determined to break through to her. 'Life's so short, Sophie. We're only given so much time. It's a crime not to live it to the full. If something good passes our way we should grab it with both hands, because before we know it we're dead.'

His words shocked her to frozen stillness. She looked at him in horror, and in the ghastly flickering light of the oncoming storm she was as white as a ghost.

There was a moment when it seemed as if the world had stopped. Then she jumped up, her hands gripping the table, and she too was shouting, hysterically.

'How can you say that to me, after what I told you the other night? If there's one thing you don't have to tell me, it's that! I know all I ever want to know about the briefness of life and the robbery of death!'

'That's exactly why I said it!' he shouted back. 'I've been kind, I've been patient, I've left you alone as you asked. I don't want to hurt you, but I will if it breaks through that shell you've put around yourself.'

They faced each other wildly. She was trembling, sick, and the thick, threatening air made her temples pound. For a minute or two the noise of the thunder stopped and there was a silence broken only by their heaving breaths.

She felt his eyes, angry, insistent, compelling, on hers, and tears formed in her throat and threatened to spill from her eyes. And she knew if they did she would be lost.

Then a sizzling hiss of lightning split the sky and in the same instant a deafening crack of thunder broke overhead. Sophie screamed and began to run blindly, bolting like a terrified fawn from the terrible noise, the dreadful churning, threatening emotion.

'Sophie!' His voice commanded her to stop but she was in total panic, running anywhere just to get away. And as she ran, down steps, along paths, over grass, the heavens opened and drenching rain soaked her to the skin in seconds.

CHAPTER THIRTEEN

SOPHIE ran and ran, with tears and rain streaming down her face and her thin dress plastered to her body. When she stumbled, she kicked away her shoes and ran barefoot. Rose thorns caught at her arms but she pulled herself free, running from Seth, from herself, her past. Yet the past was at her heels, its dark shadows looming over her, just as Seth was behind her, his voice harsh with anxiety as he called her name.

She ran until she could not run any more but collapsed, still sobbing, against the trunk of a tree. She leant her forehead against the rough bark and ground her skin hard against the tree until it hurt. Maybe this was the same tree they had played beneath this afternoon, she thought abstractedly, and wild, hysterical laughter bubbled on her lips. What would her children say if they could see their beloved Miss Walker now, crazy in the torrenting rain? They would barely recognise her.

But she no longer recognised herself, and the tears flowed again because she knew she had lost the person she had spent years so carefully rebuilding, lost her grip, lost her head . . .

'Sophie! Oh, dear heaven, Sophie, what are you doing?'

Seth was here, she could hear his running footsteps.

He was behind her, she could hear the roughness of his breath as he came closer, then his hands on her shoulders turned her round to him and he caught her close, in a hard, anguished embrace.

'Oh!'

'Oh!'

They both gasped at the contact. He was rough with her, angry with anxiety and frustration. She did not care, she did not care about anything. Ever since she decided to come tonight she had known deep down that some dam must burst, some storm break over them. Now it was beginning, and she was frightened but wildly exhilarated as well. Whatever happened now would happen because it had to, she thought, and she felt something heavy lift from her shoulders and leave her free.

He held her arms, pulled her close, pushed her back a little to see her tear-soaked face. There was so much pent-up passion in him she could feel it in his every impatient touch.

'What the hell were you doing? It's pitch black, you could have fallen. Are you all right——'

He pushed back her drenched hair. His shirt clung wetly to his body. She nodded, sobbing, pushed her head into his shoulder, needing him as she never had before.

'Oh, Sophie!' He groaned, still angry, pulling her hard against him. 'Sophie.'

His mouth found hers, cool, wet lips meeting, as the rain still fell on them and the thunder and lightning danced their stormy duet.

'No more games, Sophie.' He spoke through his kiss, a command that brooked no denial.

'No.' She held him tight, hearing his heart thump, and knew she could not keep from loving him if she tried, but his arms were even tighter about her, as if he did not trust her not to push him away and escape again.

Now he kissed her fully, hard, deep, a kiss full of pain and passion that bruised her lips and sent the blood on fire through her veins. His mouth punished hers as his hand caught her neck beneath her hair and pulled her head to keep her lips hard on his.

His anger and need set her aflame. She yielded easily to the hard length of his body, open to him, with all restraint stripped from her. Her fingers tangled in his thick hair, as they had so often longed to before, and held his head down to hers so that their kiss would have no end.

Now his lips were finding her eyes, her ears, her throat, and he gasped with desire.

With one swift movement he moved his hands down her bare shoulders, under the straps of her dress, dragging the flimsy, soaked scrap of material from her body so that she stood naked to the waist against him in the night and the rain fell on her glimmering form. She felt his desire harden as he touched her, not gently but possessively, his hands covering each full breast and his thumbs roughening the stiffening flesh until she was wild with need for him. She heard a stifled moan from her lips and her hands pulled at his back, but he had no mercy for her. Now he bent his head and his lips and tongue and teeth were exploring her nakedness, making her shiver and gasp and cry out for him. It was too much to bear, yet she wanted him never to stop.

'Seth, please, Seth.'

She tore at the buttons of his shirt, hearing a rip of cotton as she did so. Then his flesh was against hers, the glorious firm muscles and hard bones beneath. She threw away the shirt and inhaled the smell of him like the richest perfume, sliding her hands over his wet skin.

Then he pushed her down to the grass, falling with her, and the summer smell of bruised wet meadow grass rose round them as he ran his hands down the length of her, beneath the white lace of her pants, tearing it aside, covering her body with his.

'Don't ask me stop,' he got out against her mouth. 'Not this time.'

In answer she kissed him with all the frustration that was penned inside her, until he could bear no more and took her hand to touch him.

'Oh!' she gasped, and she felt him shudder beneath her fingers.

She pushed away the last of his clothes and he gathered her back to him, arms, bodies, legs entwined, and he rolled her back on to the grass, kissing her swollen lips hard until she could stand it no longer and her body was open to him and her hands were on his lips, drawing him into her.

Rain fell, forgotten, on them as he covered her body at last with his and took her quickly and keenly, driven by need to dispel all his fury and frustration. Again and again his body drove against hers and his hands caught her hips up to his, until she thought she would swell and burst against him before he had taken his fill of her.

But just as she trembled on the brink of her passion

he embraced her fiercely in his arms and held her
close, gasping out her name in a release that broke
over them both in flooding violent waves of exploding
sensation.

For a long time he lay with her, not letting her go,
not even loosening his embrace, until the rain on their
skin made them shiver and he relaxed the iron grip of
his arms. She opened her eyes slowly and looked over
his shoulder to the dark web of branches above them.
The storm was passing and faint moonlight shone
through a gauze of cloud.

He covered a breast with his hand, then cupped the
bone of her pelvis.

'Adam and Eve,' he said. 'Naked in the garden.'

His voice was light, but she sensed in it an uncer-
tainty about her that made her ache with love for him.
She longed to hold him safe and warm. She held his
shoulder and kissed him, letting him see her love, and
the joy of not having to banish her feelings was as
sweet a freedom as the release of their physical love.

'Before or after the apple?' she said, and her voice
sounded strange to her ears, roughened by his kisses.

'Oh, before, before. This is definitely Paradise! I
can't remember when I've been so happy.' He kissed
her lips again then eased himself up. 'Although for
Eden it's a little chilly. We must get back before you
catch pneumonia.'

'Like this?' She smiled as he helped her up.

'Why not? These clothes are soaking, worse than
useless. Anyway there's no one to see.'

Walking entwined through the night, their arms
around each other, it seemed quite natural. But at the
Hall, in the light spilling out on to the drive, she was

embarrassed by the blades of grass sticking to her legs, the scratches on her arms, and Seth, sensing it instantly, put his wet shirt about her shoulders.

Inside the house he led her quickly upstairs and found them both towelling robes. In the light she found it difficult to meet his eyes.

'Don't be embarrassed,' he said, gently drawing it over her shoulders. 'You're beautiful, and you've done nothing to be ashamed of.' His hands rested at her neck and his eyes were warm and loving. She melted under his look.

'To run off like that—it was so silly.'

'Something had to happen. We couldn't have gone on like that. At least I couldn't——'

'Nor me,' she confessed. But she found she had to look away from his eyes, and she knew things were not yet right between them. Their violent passion had discharged their physical tension but left them strangers, still cautious and uncertain, treading unknown ground.

He studied her for a moment, then said, 'Come and have a bath.'

'You've done so much to the house,' she said, looking around.

'It's been a long time since you were here. It's felt like a lifetime.'

He ran steaming water into the deep tub, with scented bath oil, and made her climb in, then gently soaped her all over.

As an adult she had never been looked after like this and it made her want to cry.

'What about you?' She nodded at the water.

He shook his head, smiling a little grimly. 'In a

minute. If I get in with you, you know what will happen. I need to make love to you about a million times before I've even begun to have enough of you.'

She rested her chin on her knees and looked at him sideways. He was kneeling beside the bath, his arm trailing over the side, and their eyes were level.

'Sophie——'

'Don't,' she said quickly, hearing the tone in his voice.

'We have to talk about things.'

A hundred butterflies beat their wings in her stomach.

She closed her eyes. 'Sophie,' he said, and his voice was very warn and close, 'don't you see it's because I love you? I love you, and I want things to be right between us.'

A tear squeezed out from between her lids.

'I can't bear it. I don't want to talk about the past any more.'

'Here, come on out.' He lifted her, dried her carefully, rubbing her hair. Still holding her with the towel, like a child, he said, 'Will you sleep beside me tonight, in my bed?'

She nodded. Speech had been robbed from her.

'Then wait for me there. I'll only be a moment.

Slowly she walked through to the panelled bedroom. It was the main room upstairs in the old Hall and it was beautiful. Lamps lit the polished oak and made the curtains glow with colour. The carpet under her bare toes was soft, and the silence was absolute. But there was no peace for her, not here, not anywhere, not ever.

'Now,' he said the moment he came in. She looked

at him quickly. His hair was tousled and damp, making him look younger, more vulnerable, if it were possible, more handsome. 'You said you didn't want to talk, Sophie, so you don't have to. Let me do the talking for us both. There's plenty I have to say.'

She stared at him with wide, puzzled eyes.

He looked serious, grim, and paced the room as if unsure how to begin.

'I'm feeling nervous,' he admitted, 'because you're going to think I've been interfering.' He gave her a straight, dark look. 'I *have* been interfering, prying into your life. It would be unforgivable under normal circumstances, but these are hardly normal, are they? Look, you'd better sit down, you might be in for a shock or two. Better still, get into bed and just listen.'

Mutely, apprehensively, she did as she was told.

'The other night, when you told me about Graham —I hated leaving you alone like that, Sophie, I only did it because I could see it was what you wanted. I've never felt so miserable and useless as I did walking down those stairs. When I went through the hall I saw your address book lying by the telephone. It was open at your friend Florence's number, in Manchester. I wasn't prying, it just caught my eye, but when I saw it I realised I had to find out for myself the truth of what had happened in London.'

'I told you the truth,' she protested.

'Your truth,' he said gently. 'What you believed happened.' He searched her eyes. 'I rang Florence, who couldn't have been nicer or more helpful once I'd explained myself. Have you any idea, Sophie, how worried all your friends have been about you?'

She shook her head slowly against the pillows.

'She told me her version of events, which didn't exactly tally with yours, even though you were sharing the same flat. For one thing, she said that even when you were all students together, long before you and Graham were engaged, Graham had complained to her about being tired and seeming to have no energy. She was also able to remember the name of his doctor, and I went up to London to see him.'

'Dr Farrell?' Sophie gasped with astonishment.

'Yes, I had no idea when I asked to see him that he had been your doctor as well, but that proved to be a fantastic stroke of luck because when I explained why I wanted to know about Graham's illness, he was only too happy to help. Do you know what he said about you?'

She shook her head.

'He said, "That young girl had the courage and strength of a woman three times her age. She knew that lad of hers didn't want to go into hospital, and she fought us tooth and nail to keep him in his own home." He said he hadn't wanted you to nurse him, that he feared the burden would be far too much for you, but that you did a superb job.'

'But he doesn't know the truth of it,' she said bitterly. There were tears in her eyes.

Seth came and put his arm round her, lifting her miserable face to his.

'I explained to him what you thought, that you felt it was somehow your fault. He said you couldn't be more wrong. For one thing, there is not the slightest evidence of any psychological cause for the illness. The latest research seems to indicate some hereditary or environmental factor that upsets the body's biochemistry. What your friend the nurse told you was quite wrong.

'The other thing is that this illness only shows itself some years after the patient has contracted it. It progresses very, very slowly at first, so that the only signs of it are a general weakness and tiredness. Graham, sad to say, would have already been a marked man by the time you met him.

'As for his having nothing to live for—well, Dr Farrell told me he'd never heard of anyone being able to throw the disease off, or even prolong their life, simply by wanting to do so. It isn't like any of those illnesses that do seem to respond to positive thinking. I'm afraid that your feelings for Graham, one way or another, would have had absolutely no impact whatever on the course of his illness.'

She stayed still in the circle of Seth's arms, waiting for the meaning of his words sink down to her brain.

'He was a good doctor,' she whispered finally. 'Maybe I should have talked to him more at the time.'

'He would like to talk to you now, if you would go up to London to see him. He said he had no idea you felt that way, and was very cross with himself for not supporting you more at the time.'

'He did what he could. He was always so busy.'

'I think you should go,' Seth said. 'It would be a good thing to hear it all directly from him.'

'Yes, I will. I can hardly believe it.'

'You didn't mind?' he asked her anxiously. 'About me prying into your life?'

'No, oh, no. I can see that I got everything twisted up in my mind.'

'It's not surprising. It was an intolerable burden to

have to bear, at such an age. And you've been brooding on it ever since.'

'Yes, I have,' she admitted. 'It's been like a black sky over my life.' She frowned. 'It still is, in a way. I can't seem to take in what you've told me.'

'It's bound to take time. And you need to talk. To Dr Farrell—to me. Sophie,' he held her closer, 'you're not alone any more, do you understand? You'll never be alone again. Lean on me, let me help you, I've got the strength to shoulder your burdens.'

His words were as luxurious as the soft pillows that cushioned her. She sighed and felt something begin to loosen within her, as the tight knot of her tension started to ease.

'You're no murderess, Sophie, you have to accept that. You didn't kill Graham, and you didn't help him die. You cared for him, and nursed him as well as you were able. No one could have done more. Once you accept that fully then you'll be able to start leaving the past behind.'

'I wish I could have loved him, though,' she said in a small voice. 'That's what he wanted.'

'It isn't in our power to decide who we'll love, and who we won't.' He turned her to him, moulding her shoulders. 'I wasn't planning to fall in love with you, yet it happened. I think it happened that very first night, maybe even the first moment you walked into the room.'

'I just lived through my work. It was the only part of my life that felt unsullied. I vowed I would never get involved with anyone again. I knew I didn't deserve anyone's love. That's why I couldn't bear the way you pursued me.'

'Oh, Sophie!' There was anguish in his voice. 'If I'd had any idea what you were going through—I didn't understand, not any of it. There was such a pull between us, right from that first night, and yet you froze me out so completely. That evening I came to your house, after the inspectors had been at the school, I knew I was taking advantage of you. It was clear how much stress you'd been under, and I could see exactly how the champagne was going to your head, yet I kept on refilling your glass. I thought if I could storm your defences, maybe take you to bed, then you would have to open up to me.'

'I wanted you so much. It was only because you stopped——'

'I felt so protective of you, all the time. The last thing I wanted was to give you a baby against your wishes.' He grimaced. 'Although tonight——'

She buried her head in his arms. 'I want your babies. It was agony seeing you those times and not being able to reach out to you. I used to lie awake all night after one of our friendly outings, thinking about you.'

He eased her back and looked with warmth into her eyes.

'Do you have any more secrets for me, Sophie Walker, before I carry you off and make you my bride?'

She pondered the muddle of her recent life, as a prospect of true happiness unfolded before her.

'I applied for the headship of the school last month, but they turned me down,' she confessed. 'At the interview I was accused of having men staying with me.' She smiled ruefully.

'Did I wreck your chances?'

'No, I would have been too young anyway.'

'I wouldn't have cared if I had. I want you to myself —for a few years at least. When we've had our honeymoon and made our home here, and Sedbury Hall is full of children, then you can carry on up your career ladder.'

She looked deep into his eyes. 'I can't take it in. I thought I would be alone for ever, yet you came along and walked straight through my defences.'

'Sophie, I love you. I love you so much it hurts, and nothing you've said to me has altered that one bit. All it has done is explain a lot of mysteries.' His hands gently stroked her hair, her neck, and as she looked at him she felt a great peace welling up in her heart. A weight had been taken from her, and she was at long last able to meet his eyes free from guilt and fear.

'I love you, too, Seth, I think I always have done, although I would not admit it to myself. I was too scared, too frightened of where it might lead.'

His hands held her head and he kissed her gently and completely.

'It leads here, to this house, this room, this bed. To us. It leads to marriage and children, to your work and mine, to us always being together . . .'

'Yes,' she said. 'Yes.'

Gently he eased her back against the pillows, and with a long kiss of love and understanding their life together began.

ROMANCING
THE PHONE

Win the romantic holiday of a lifetime for two at the exclusive Couples Hotel in Ocho Rios on Jamaica's north coast with the Mills & Boon and British Telecom's novel competition, 'Romancing the Phone'.

This exciting competition looks at the importance the telephone call plays in romance. All you have to do is write a story or extract about a romance involving the phone which lasts approximately two minutes when read aloud.

The winner will not only receive the holiday in Jamaica, but the entry will also be heard by millions of people when it is included in a selection of extracts from a short list of entries on British Telecom's 'Romance Line'. Regional winners and runners up will receive British Telecom telephones, answer machines and Mills & Boon books.

For an entry leaflet and further details all you have to do is call 01 400 5359, or write to 'Romancing the Phone', 22 Endell Street, London WC2H 9AD.
You may be mailed with other offers as a result of this application.

Unwrap romance this Christmas

A Love Affair
LINDSAY ARMSTRONG

Valentine's Night
PENNY JORDAN

Man on the Make
ROBERTA LEIGH

Rendezvous in Rio
ELIZABETH OLDFIELD

Put some more romance into your Christmas, with four brand new titles from Mills & Boon in this stylish gift pack.

They make great holiday reading, and for only £5.40, it makes an ideal gift.

The special gift pack is available from 6th October. Look out for it at Boots, Martins, John Menzies, W.H. Smith, Woolworths and other paperback stockists.